SOUL
CAPTAINS

This book is dedicated to my first-born, Henry Edward Sparling.
His short and cherished life inspires his parents every day.

First published in Australia in 2022
by Atlantis Books
Suite 83/20-40 Meagher Street
Chippendale
NSW 2008
www.littlesteps.com.au
www.atlantisbooks.com.au

A Catalogue-In-Publication entry for this book is
available from the National Library of Australia.

ISBN: 978-1-922678-68-3

Designed by Nina Nielsen

Printed in China

10 9 8 7 6 5 4 3 2 1

SOUL CAPTAINS

BY WILLIAM SPARLING

Atlantis Books

PROLOGUE

The yellow and orange liquid was a hideous sight. Bits of ham and corn protruded from it, making it look like some kind of tropical reef plant. Flies battled over it for supremacy like it was liquid gold. Their buzzing sounds grew louder with each passing second.

The smell was worse–akin to an old piece of fish that had been left in the fridge far too long, mixed with pig brain. The odour alone was enough to make someone sick.

Valour stared at the vomit in the latrine bowl, clutching his stomach. He wiped a fly from his face, beads of sweat pouring off. His fingernails were covered in dirt.

He closed his eyes, wishing he were somewhere, anywhere else.

What have I done to deserve this? he wondered. It felt like a demon had entered his body and decided to do somersaults.

He'd been kissing the toilet bowl for the best part of an hour.

He knew he should have avoided lunch. His stomach had been upset that morning, but he'd thought having a hearty meal would prepare him for the mission that afternoon.

He tried to distract himself by imagining being back home on the beach, relaxing among the waves on a summer's day. The cool water and the warmth of the sunshine were a perfect mix. The golden sand provided an oasis-like atmosphere. Body boarding with his daughter brought a smile to his face. It was their shared passion.

His unforgiving, grumbling stomach soon interrupted his thoughts.

He opened his eyes and stared back at his lunch. The stench was overwhelming. His mouth opened wide, as he regurgitated what was left in his stomach before collapsing on the floor of the latrine.

He felt like a failure. He had been trained as a warrior, able to fend off any enemy. Yet here he was, struggling like an animal on its last legs, barely able to fend off flies.

Heavy metal music sang out across that section of the army base. He hated it. Sounded like an idiot banging sticks on a drum set, alongside an even bigger idiot yelling something incoherent into a microphone.

Maybe that was the army's new strategy to combat the Taliban — death by useless music. The enemy must think Westerners are mad — listening to this ear-aching nonsense.

This was followed by the sound of military helicopters hovering high above. They were a common sight and sound in this part of the world.

This time though, the sound caused his heart to beat furiously. That morning, two choppers had returned three soldiers to base—two dead and one seriously wounded.

Seeing the blood-soaked stretchers and the screams from the surviving soldier reminded Valour of the realities of war. Nothing could be taken for granted.

The sound of their monstrous propellers caused Valour's body to tremble. He placed his hands over his ears, attempting to block out the noise. All he wanted was silence. The other soldiers loved the sound. They thought it brought their bones to life and motivated them before a big mission.

He used what energy he had left to sit up and rest his back on the side of the latrine door. He filled his mind with happier thoughts – his wife, daughter and the life they'd built together.

He breathed heavily and sighed. He'd travelled thousands of kilometres to fight the Taliban in Afghanistan – a country most people couldn't even locate on a map – yet on this occasion his enemy was food poisoning.

'You okay in there, mate?' a voice called out from the other side of the door.

Valour recognised the voice. It was his platoon buddy, Pete.

He shook his head. 'Yeah, I'll be okay. Just give me a minute.'

'You can be the one who cleans the latrines next time round, since you've caused the damage,' Pete sniggered, before walking off and laughing.

'Bloody loser,' Valour whispered to himself before stumbling to his feet in a dizzying manner. Latrine duty was by far the worst task on base. All soldiers dreaded seeing their name on the roster.

While most enlisted into the army with dreams of serving Australia with pride and embodying the Anzac spirit, some responsibilities, despite how grotesque, couldn't be avoided.

He rotated his head from side to side, wiped his mouth with his sleeve and then took one last look at the putrid sight, before putting the toilet lid down. He still felt nauseous but at least the demon was out of his system.

He washed his hands, splashed water over his clean-shaven face and opened the latrine door.

The sweltering heat felt like a slap in the face. The sun's rays were intense and unforgiving. There wasn't a cloud in the sky. There never was these days. Every day in summer seemed to bring blistering heat.

Despite being exhausted following patrols, soldiers found it difficult to sleep in this oven-like environment.

It was about 35 degrees Celsius in the shade. He wiped sweat from his hair, which was an archetypal military style haircut – extremely short on the back and sides and only slightly longer on top.

A furry figure rubbed against his legs, panting. It was Sapper, his black Labrador. His black fur coat was littered with dust. He was no pet though. He was a war dog who had undergone rigorous training back home. Valour considered him a part of his soul.

'I hear you, boy, let's get you some water.'

He glanced at his silver wedding ring, which shone brightly on his left hand. Marrying Veronica was the happiest day in his life. The love of his life. The love and warmth from reliving that day helped overcome the nausea he was feeling.

Valour retrieved sunglasses from his pocket and placed them over his eyes, adjusted his desert camouflage uniform and started to walk.

Grey and brown dirt crunched under his tan coloured boots as he made his way towards the outdoor gym. He heard that crunching sound wherever he went. It was a defining feature of this complex country.

Sapper followed next to him, tail wagging.

The Australian flag flew above the entrance to the base, which was heavily fortified with barbed wire and two soldiers, armed with rifles, on lookout. They looked like prison guards, unafraid of knocking off an inmate, or in this case an intruder.

About eighty metres away was the mess tent for meals. Soldiers gathered on long tables, chewing into their meals like hyenas, only coming up for breath once in a while.

He passed two giant camouflage coloured Bushmaster all-wheel-drive vehicles. Beasts on wheels, capable of defending soldiers against improvised explosive devices and enemy fire. An icon of Australia's Afghanistan war effort.

Valour was literally in the middle of nowhere. A place called Tarin Kowt in the Uruzgan Province of southern Afghanistan. An ancient town that seemed content living in the biblical age, with its dusty village markets alongside dirt roads, women covered head to toe, and the most humble homes you could ever imagine.

The landscape was defined by kilometres of arid desert, with sections of oasis like green flora and mountain ranges.

The polar opposite of suburban Australia.

The army base he was stationed on wasn't always the polar opposite. It could often feel like a gated community, shut off from the rest of Tarin Kowt, with its gym, sleeping quarters, modern music and regular supply of food.

The unbearable heavy metal music grew louder with every stride. A boom box that was the source of the repulsive sounds sat next to a man using a bench press in the outdoor gym.

'Ninety-eight, ninety-nine, one hundred,' the man said proudly with ease, as he completed a heavy set of bench pressing. The man sat up, breathing heavily and winked at Valour. Veins almost burst out of his muscular arms.

'Yeah right, as if you can do more than ten, mate,' Valour said, turning down the music.

Jimmy stood up and laughed, running his hands through his sweaty blonde hair. His singlet was covered in perspiration. Despite being a few inches shorter than Valour, he looked just as strong. He had a confident swagger about him like that of a professional athlete. Head always held high, his face always seemed to wear a permanent smile.

He'd always been a talented sportsman. Top sprinter at school, captain of the athletics team. He was a driven sort of guy. You knew when he set himself a goal, he'd achieve it.

He was also a great mate. When Valour's father died when they were in Year 10, Jimmy checked up on him every day, even if they just sat in silence. He was there, a constant he needed in life. He still couldn't believe he outranked Jimmy in the army.

'What's the point of having guns like these if I'm not going to show them off?' he boasted, shaking his arms.

Jimmy continued. 'As if you'd know anything. Can you even see me from the latrine, mate?' he asked, patting Valour on his left shoulder. 'Looks and sounds like you've been practising your lunges over there. Hope you got it all out. The last thing your platoon needs this afternoon is you spewing up your guts while on patrol.'

'You reckon?' Valour asked sarcastically, rolling his eyes. 'Can you at least offer Sapper some water?' pointing to the water bottle sitting next to a dumb bell.

'Yeah, of course,' Jimmy said, handing Valour the bottle. 'Gotta look after our four-legged life saver.'

The pair watched on with amusement as Sapper drank from Valour's hand as he held the bottle above his head, allowing the water to flow down. How could something so unsophisticated looking be so revered? they pondered.

'All that water makes me want to surf,' Jimmy said, smiling.

Valour chuckled. 'You do realise we're in a landlocked country, right?

'Yeah, fair point. At least I can work on my tan in this heat though. Remind me, how many bombs has Sapper detected so far on this tour?'

Valour looked down at his mate, patting him on the head. 'Ten and counting. That's at least ten lives and villages saved so far.'

'Yeah, maths was never your strongest subject at school, but that seems to add up. Damn he's good!' Jimmy exclaimed.

'So I've got some news I'd like to share.'

'Oh yeah, what's that, mate?' Valour asked curiously. 'You've turned your six pack into an eight pack?'

'Ha ha, very funny,' Jimmy replied. 'If you must know I've already achieved that. My actual news is that this muscular, super fit dad of two is about to become a dad of three.'

'Woo hoo!' Valour yelled, opening his arms wide to embrace his friend. 'I'm so happy for you guys,' he said, while hugging his mate.

'Okay, Okay, enough of the cuddling,' Jimmy said, pulling himself off him. 'We're certainly excited. Though my life is about to get even busier, if that's even possible.'

'When are you guys expecting?'

'Six months, mate. It's going to fly. Jenny and Victoria will have a baby brother or sister to look after. You can help change the nappies this time around as well. Don't recall you offering last time.'

'I think I'd rather put my hand up for another tour than do that, mate,' Valour said.

The pair burst out laughing.

'Are you two laughing at me?' a voice called out from close range.

The pair recognised the deep, crackly tone. It was their Commanding Officer Reg Samson. He had a towering and intimidating presence about him – tall, broad shoulders, razor thin haircut.

'No sir,' they both said in a synchronised way, while standing to attention.

'At ease, fellas,' Samson said.

Samson approached Valour, just inches from his face. He looked him squarely in the eye. He was known for being a straight shooter.

He was also a soldier's soldier. He'd served two tours in Afghanistan, one in Iraq and was highly decorated. He was physically and mentally tough. The type of person who others look up to.

'Now Corporal, I hear you're unwell. Is that true?'

Valour looked him squarely in the eye before responding. 'Yes sir, got a bout of food poisoning from lunch but I'll be okay. You know me. Nothing can stop me going out on patrol.'

'Well, it appears lunch has stopped you on this occasion,' Samson explained. 'We cannot risk having you fall ill while on patrol. We need our soldiers to be one hundred per cent battle ready and you, sir, are not. Rest up today and let's see how you feel tomorrow.'

Valour's stomach felt like it was caught in a knot. Not from the illness but a feeling of guilt and despair.

'Please sir, it's not that bad,' he begged. 'It's all out of the system. I'm better now. I don't want to let the team down. I can do it.'

Samson shook his head. 'Sorry, Corporal, it's out of my hands. I'm just following the rule book. Also means your four-legged warrior has to remain here as well.'

He turned to face Jimmy. 'Lance Corporal, I need you to fill in for the Corporal. Do you think you can manage that?'

'Yes sir,' Jimmy replied.

'Good to hear,' Samson said. 'Don't worry, I'm told there shouldn't be too much action this afternoon.'

Valour waited for his Commanding Officer to be out of sight before talking.

'I'm so sorry, mate, I know you're supposed to have

this afternoon off. It's all my fault.'

'Don't sweat it,' Jimmy said. 'These things happen. Plus, the last thing local Afghans need to see is you spewing your guts up in their villages. Rest up this afternoon. Samson is a cranky old fart. Don't challenge him.'

'Yeah, I know,' Valour said. 'I swear steam comes out of his nostrils when he speaks.'

'Sure does, but he knows his stuff, mate. He's been on so many tours. He understands these villages and the enemy better than any of us. We're in good hands.'

While Jimmy went out on patrol that afternoon, Valour rested on his stretcher bed in the accommodation tent reserved for Non-Commissioned Officers. Rows of makeshift stretcher beds lined each side of the room. The floor was wooden.

It was hot inside and his body felt sticky from sweat. He drifted in and out of sleep before deciding to write an email back home.

Valour removed his iPad from his duffle bag and checked his email inbox. He'd received an email from his daughter that morning. Valour hadn't heard from her in a few days and opened the email with enthusiasm.

Hi Dad,

Hope this email finds you well. How is everything over there? Is Sapper looking after you?

I've been watching stories about the war on the TV news. Sounds pretty rough. Stay safe.

Wish you were here. I have some news! We won the local girls' soccer tournament. First time in 15 years. To top it off, I scored the only goal in the entire game and was named player of the match.

Mum was cheering me on from the sidelines, but she's nowhere near as loud as you are.

Although you weren't there, I know you were there in spirit.

Also got my mid-year school report card. Three As this time. My best yet. Even got an A in maths. Can you believe it?

I took your advice and have been helping Mum more around the house. Taught myself how to mow the lawn. Must admit, it took a bit of getting used to. The first time I did it, it was so uneven.

I'm also taking the bins out every week, setting the table before dinner and helping with cleaning.

Can't say I enjoy it, but if it makes Mum's life a bit easier and makes you happy, then I'm fine with it.

You can be rest assured I'm eating well. Even though

*you're not here I can still imagine you reminding me
of how breakfast is the most important meal of the day.
Don't worry, I've been eating a hearty brekkie every day.
Anyway, just wanted to touch base and share my
news with you. I cuddle the teddy bear you left me
with the letter 'M' on its belly.*

Hope Jimmy isn't causing too much drama.

Love you.
Your favourite daughter xox

Valour grinned at the screen. It was the best he'd felt
all week. He missed his daughter so much.

He clicked reply and proceeded to type an email back.

Dear sweetie,

*So lovely to hear from you. Things have been okay
over here. It's ridiculously hot. Feels like I'm stuck in
an oven all day.*

*I go out patrolling with my platoon most days. Sapper
keeps me on my toes. I don't know where he finds the
energy. He's become a hit with the locals. They think
he's some sort of special dog when he walks around
villages wearing his cool little boots to protect his feet.
It's tough work but I enjoy it. Feel like I'm helping*

Afghans by keeping them safe.

I've made friends with some locals. I've become friends with a man named Abdul who is an Afghan interpreter attached to our platoon. He's married to a lovely lady named Mariam who is obsessed with cricket. I'm sure you'd be delighted to hear that lol.

Congrats on winning the soccer tournament. Better watch out – next you know you'll have an English Premier League club recruiting you.

Three As! That's three more than I ever got. Since when did you become so well rounded? Are you sure you're my daughter?

I'm so proud of you.

Don't worry, Uncle Jimmy is being his usual self. I think he spends more time at the gym on base here than he does back home, if you can believe that. Such a random guy haha.

Say hi to your mum for me. Miss you both so much.

Talk soon.
Love Dad xoxox

Valour then opened a new email and composed an email for his wife.

Dear Veronica,

Hope you're well. I've been a bit rotten today. Must have been something I ate. My Commanding Officer wouldn't even let me go on today's patrol. Jimmy had to cover for me.

Did you hear the news? Jimmy and Michelle are expecting their third child. So happy for them.

I miss you so much. Despite how hard it is over here I get through it by thinking of you both. Counting down the days until we're united as a family again.

Sounds like our daughter is kicking goals on and off the field. I'm one proud dad!

Take care.

Love Valour xox

He turned the tablet off, packed it away and lay down on his bed. He stared at the green canvas roof for a few minutes and fell asleep.

He woke a couple of hours later to noise and commotion. A helicopter could be heard landing nearby.

There seemed to be a lot of anguish, with fellow soldiers yelling with urgency.

The tent door flung open and a figure appeared

inside. It was his Commanding Officer.

'Corporal, have you got a minute to chat?' he asked, expressionless.

Valour felt a sense of worry and unease flow through his body. A shiver went down his spine.

It would be the hardest conversation of his life. His life would never be the same again.

CHAPTER 1

Veronica lay in bed staring at the ceiling. She'd been awake fifteen minutes. Nothing special, just a white ceiling with a few cracks. She and her husband used to joke that they would one day wake up and find themselves buried under a pile of rubble.

Nowadays she sometimes wished those cracks would grow larger and crack and crumble, putting her out of her misery.

She looked across to the right side of the bed. It was empty. She refused to sleep there. That was her husband's spot. Despite him being gone, she liked to remember him by leaving some things as they were.

During nights when she turned in her sleep, she would still do it discreetly without making too much movement or noise, so she didn't disturb him.

The weight of responsibilities she carried always outweighed the inner sadness she felt and gave her the strength to get out of bed every day.

She opened her mouth wide and acted like she was screaming but without making a sound. She did that most mornings nowadays.

She grabbed her mobile phone from the bedside

table and looked at the time. It read 6.30am. Next to her phone was a framed photo of the couple on their wedding day. Felt like an eternity ago now.

The photo was covered in dust. The house had been neglected for some time and was in need of some love. The wall paint was fading and the kitchen sink leaked.

Her husband was the handy man who could fix everything.

Thinking of that day always brought a smile to her face. It was a beautiful day – clear blue sky and warm.

They even used similar wording in their vows, with both saying they would be there for each other through the good and the bad and nothing was too challenging to overcome together.

Although these days, she felt like an imposter. Vows are easier said than done. Even though all couples inevitably face hardships, all pray they never have to endure any. They all want that movie style picturesque wedding where you have children and live happily ever after in a nice house.

But life isn't a movie and it's not always picturesque, as Veronica discovered.

She covered her face with her hands and sighed.

'Time to get started,' she whispered to herself, before climbing out of bed.

She made her bed, had a shower, ate breakfast

and got started on folding clean laundry back in her bedroom.

The bedroom was her default place to be. A lot of significant life moments and conversations had taken place in that room, and it was filled with memories.

It was where she told her husband she was pregnant, where he told her each time he had to go on a tour of duty to Afghanistan and where they engaged in many arguments about his life post-army.

She was a stickler for neatness and made sure the t-shirts, pyjamas, bed sheets and pants were so neatly piled up you felt guilty for unfolding them.

Being meticulous was part of her DNA. She'd been raised in a strict Chinese Australian family where perfection was an achievable target.

Anything less than an A was below average.

She worked hard throughout her adolescence and achieved greatness — Dux, school captain, head army cadet, opening batsman for the first XI cricket team and a top pianist.

This was followed by a full scholarship to study accounting at university. She lived a perfect life, met the man of her dreams, got married, had a baby and raised her family in a quintessential suburban neighbourhood.

Veronica considered herself a tiger mum — a strong

disciplinarian who could be tough and fair. She wanted the best for her daughter Maple and thought that the best way to raise her was to mould her into a junior version of herself. If it worked for her, then it should work for her daughter. Or so she thought.

It didn't all go as planned.

She looked out the window. Her once beautiful backyard lawn was now overgrown and filled with weeds. Hadn't been mown in months. The garden bed was as good as dead.

While placing t-shirts in a drawer, the sight of her husband's army ceremonial uniform caught her attention. It was khaki green coloured with medals still attached to the jacket's left breast pocket.

She'd left her husband's section of the wardrobe the same. She didn't have the courage to throw his things out or store them elsewhere. Keeping everything in place provided Veronica with a sense of hope. As each day passed by, it seemed more like a false sense of hope.

Veronica ran her right hand over the medals. She didn't know the difference between them but knew he must have done something special to earn them.

The collar still smelled of his cologne. It's what she smelt whenever they hugged each other. She brushed specks of dust off the shoulders.

Tears wet her cheeks. All Veronica wanted was to have him back, to hold him again. A part of her soul left that day when he left, but she had to put on a brave face and soldier on for the sake of their daughter.

Staring back at the medals, Veronica wished she knew more about them and their meanings. How could such a small bit of metal cause so much grief and agony? They didn't include that in the enlistment information pack.

Only images of warriors dressed head to toe in camouflage, fighting for their country and defending the Anzac tradition.

None of the TV ads ever mentioned the invisible wounds of war and the toll they take on military families. Seemed like misleading advertising.

She never wanted Maple to enlist. Sounded like the worst possible career move. Giving the military your heart and soul and in return them giving you false hope and a dysfunctional family. Pretty poor return on investment.

She wiped away the tears and walked over to the bedside table and opened the drawer.

She picked up an envelope and removed a letter. It was the letter her husband left for her the day he walked out.

Veronica had read it thousands of times before

but constantly felt the need to re-read it, in case she'd missed any signs or clues.

My dearest Veronica,

I never thought I would be writing you such a letter. We've built such an amazing life and family together. I thought I was stronger and better than this. I feel so weak having to write words on a page rather than having the courage to say them to your face.

The past few years have been a rollercoaster, with more downs than ups. Although I may have the physical strength to carry on, my mind and soul is somewhere else and I cannot be the husband you deserve or the father our daughter needs by being here.

This has nothing to do with you. It is entirely my fault. I have failed as a husband and father. Having me around will only cause further distress and dysfunction.

You are both better off without me. You may not see that now but you will over time. I'm a broken man. What our family needs is stability which is something I cannot provide.

I'm doing this to protect you. You may not realise this now but over time I'm sure you'll reflect and agree it was the right decision.

You deserve to be happy and constantly smiling, yet I feel my presence has the opposite effect.

Don't come looking for me. I'm in a better place. I'm finding peace. I've got the dog with me so I'll be okay. We'll look out for each other.

This is goodbye. I'm hopeful that my departure will reawaken a part of you that has been absent for some time and you chase your dreams.

You'll always be in my heart. The memories I've shared with you over the years will be my guiding light going forward.

Love Valour.

Veronica folded the letter, placed it back in the drawer and slammed it shut causing the bedside table to move.

Her tears were replaced with anger. Her blood boiled as she repeated some of the sentences from the letter in her head. She clenched her fists and punched the bed in frustration. She repeated the action a few times, hoping it would bring relief.

'I hate you! I hate you!' she screamed, continuing to punch the bed. 'You have the guts to go to war but can't even provide for your family. You're hopeless. How could you pack up and leave your wife and daughter

24

behind? What type of father does that? We're better off without you.'

She looked back at their wedding photo and put it in the drawer with the letter. She didn't want to be reminded of him.

She looked at her hands. The diamonds in her wedding ring glittered. She wore it from time to time. It served as a promise to herself that each passing day was one day closer to having him back in her life.

She removed the ring and placed it alongside the wedding photo.

She sat at the edge of the bed. She always thought marrying Valour was the best decision she ever made. Now she doubted it. Was it the worst? Could she have foreseen this? Valour's dad experienced similar struggles after returning from the Vietnam War.

He was never the same. Constantly had nightmares, the smallest things would make him aggressive and he drank way too much. His marriage eventually broke down and he died a relatively young man. So much potential wasted. His mind and conscience had been left behind in some jungle in Vietnam.

Seemed like Valour's had been left behind in a dusty village in Afghanistan.

How did it all come to this? she wondered.

Veronica ran her fingers through her shoulder

length black hair and stood up.

She walked to the bedroom mirror and stared at herself. There were more and more grey hairs. She couldn't remember the last time she applied make-up to her face. That would require her to go out and have a life once in a while.

'What have you done to yourself?' she whispered to herself. 'You must be stronger.'

She turned and walked towards the door.

'Focus, focus,' she said, while walking out of the bedroom.

Despite her challenges, she was still a mother.

She walked down the hallway and knocked on a bedroom door. 'Wake up honey, you need to get ready for school.' She waited a few moments. No response.

She knocked again. Still no response.

'Alright, I'm coming in.'

Veronica opened the door. Maple was fast asleep. She had her back to Veronica and snored quietly.

Although Maple was sixteen-years-old, Veronica always thought of her as her cub. She stood still for a minute admiring the sight. So peaceful and innocent. Almost made life's other challenges worthwhile.

The walls were covered in images – posters of a female rock band, the captain of the Matildas soccer team and a photo of her with her dad when she was nine.

Next to a desk was a shelf lined with trophies she's been awarded for her soccer accomplishments. Even though she knew what they said, Veronica still enjoyed reading the engraving on each.

She approached the shelf and leaned forward. 'Most Valuable Player' one read, while another said 'Best and Fairest Player.' It brought a smile to her face.

She looked down at her daughter and wondered where it all went wrong. Where had that innocent girl gone?

'Time to get up, otherwise you'll be late. Now come on,' she pleaded.

'Go away, leave me alone. I just want to sleep,' Maple objected, waving her right arm around in protest.

'No, it's time, Maple, now get up.' Veronica pulled her blanket and top sheet off.

'You're so annoying!' Maple barked, shrivelling up like a ball to stay warm.

'You can't stay in that position forever. Hurry up and get ready.'

Maple sat up looking groggy after a long sleep. She wiped her eyes and yawned.

'Now go have a shower, put your uniform on and come down for breakfast.'

'Yeah whatever, boss.'

She used to be such a morning person, the first to

jump out of bed full of energy and enthusiasm for the day ahead.

Each day now seemed like a struggle and burden.

Maple stood in the shower, her head facing the water. She wished the water would rinse her of her anger and frustration. Cleanse her.

Mould was visible in every corner of the shower. It spread further each week.

'This place is disgusting,' she said.

She turned the shower off and grabbed a towel. She looked down at her hands and feet. Water continued to run down her legs. Her left fingernails and toenails were painted black, while those on her right were painted green. The camouflage colours were a way for her to remember her dad's military service. No one else understood.

Other girls at school thought it looked ugly and masculine, garnering her the nickname Major Maple. Some even saluted her at school.

She didn't care. The old Maple would have become paranoid and worked up about such a thing, but the new Maple couldn't care less what others thought. She was in her own little world.

She wrapped her towel around her body and looked in the mirror. She was half Caucasian and half Chinese. Being different didn't bother her when she was younger, but as she got older it could be confusing. Her mother was a strict disciplinarian, the product of a conservative Chinese family. This was in stark contrast to her dad, who was laid back and spent his childhood holidays travelling around the country with his parents in their caravan.

She didn't know who she really was.

She was an only child. Growing up, she liked it–spoiled rotten, always the centre of attention.

Nowadays, she was the only one in the firing line. The only person her mother could rely on to help out.

Her black hair was shoulder length, like her mum. These days, it was the only similarity they shared.

Maple looked at the red pimple on her left cheek. She'd seen it the day before. It had grown a bit larger and looked like a mini volcano on her face.

The old Maple would have squeezed it and let the volcano explode, then applied make-up. The new Maple didn't care. She was happy for the volcano to grow.

She walked back to her bedroom and got dressed. Her school uniform consisted of a short-sleeved white shirt, dark blue skirt, with white socks and black shoes.

She approached the soccer trophies on the shelf and turned them around so you couldn't read the engraving. She didn't want to be reminded of that life.

Her stomach grumbled. She was hungry but couldn't bear the thought of having to engage in meaningless conversation with her mum over breakfast.

She grabbed her black backpack and the body board resting against the wall, and walked down the hallway towards the front door.

'Where do you think you're going, young lady?' her mother enquired, just as Maple reached the front door.

Maple turned around with a stern look in her eyes and grinding her teeth.

'Off to school, silly. Have a nice day sitting around doing nothing.'

Veronica shook her head and pointed at her. 'You forgot to take the bins out again last night. This is getting ridiculous. I reminded you over and over again yesterday. You don't listen.'

'Cut me some slack,' Maple replied. 'I had a ton of homework last night and forgot. I'll remember next time.'

Maple eagerly grabbed the door handle, keen to get out.

'You just wait there, Maple. Go have some breakfast. I've made you muesli and fruit. You need the energy. Maple rolled her eyes. 'I'll get something on the way.

You don't need to worry. Just worry about yourself.'

'You can't keep eating that fast food junk. You need something healthier. Come and sit down. What are doing with the body board? You're not going to the beach after school.'

'I'll eat here tomorrow, just give me a break today. I won't be at the beach long. It's summer. Everyone is there.'

Veronica raised her mobile phone in her right hand. 'Your old soccer coach, Mr Wilson, called again. He said you're always welcome back on the team. They could do with your right foot. They've been missing it. The team is dropping down the ladder.'

'Care factor zero,' Maple said. 'What's the point? It's just school soccer. It's not like I'm going off to play in the professional league. These people are obsessed. They should go and find someone else to fill my role.'

'That attitude won't get you anywhere. You've got a talent,' Veronica said. 'Don't waste it. Your coach reckons you've got what it takes to go all the way and play professionally. Why are you throwing away so much potential? When I was your age I …'

Maple interrupted her mum before she could finish her sentence. 'Oh, here we go again. It's all about you, as usual. Perfect Veronica, best at everything. You don't get it, Mum. I don't want to live in your shadow.

I want to live my own life, not relive yours. I bet you want me to go professional so we can move out of this dump and to somewhere nicer. Anyway, what would the coach know? He never made it very far. He was just an amateur.'

'I didn't mean that,' Veronica said. 'You just need to focus on something. Anything. Your father would want you to be happy.'

'How would you know?' Maple asked, raising her voice. 'He left us, Mum. He doesn't care about us. If he did, he'd still be here. I'm not surprised he left, with you constantly putting us under your microscope.'

Tears filled Veronica's eyes. 'Keep your voice down. You've got no idea. Alright, just leave then. We'll talk later. We also need to talk about your most recent report card. You've gone from being an A student to a C student. Now isn't the time to slack off. The next couple of years are the most important and will help determine your future. Don't throw it away.'

'Oh yeah, perfect Veronica always got straight As. Veronica would never let her family down by getting a C. You're so lame.'

'Just go Maple, if you insist on being unpleasant. We'll talk later and hopefully you'll be in a better mood.'

Maple grunted, before leaving and slamming the door behind her. She couldn't wait to get out.

Veronica placed her face in her hands and sobbed. She worried about her daughter. She used to love boasting to her friends about how well rounded she was. Keeping up with Maple's commitments gave her a routine as well. All she wanted was to see her daughter be happy and realise her potential.

CHAPTER 2

Maple felt like yelling at the top of her lungs to help rid her of the anger, but doing so would bring unwanted attention. The last thing she wanted was attention.

Arguing with her mum had become almost a daily ritual. Using her as a verbal boxing bag was a way to get her day's emotional baggage off her chest.

She took a deep breath, flung the body board over her shoulder and walked down the front steps and looked back over her shoulder. Her face had turned pink from the bickering and arguing.

The front door had a red poppy flower stuck to it. It had faded a bit over the years, like the rest of the house. It was a constant reminder of their life, past and present. That one small flower symbolised the rollercoaster that was her family – defined by service, sacrifice, heartache, loss and perseverance.

She and her mum were what's called a poppy family – the family of a war veteran. They were the only house in the street with one.

Perhaps no one else in the street was dumb enough to enlist. They'd seen enough news reports and movies depicting the brutal realities of war, both on the battlefront and home front, to know the risks and to avoid them.

Good men and women had joined in good faith, then been sent to a country most people would struggle to spell, let alone pinpoint on a map, only to return leaving behind a limb or their mind.

Why would they give their hearts, souls and in some cases their lives, to an institution and war, that in return gives their families endless doses of dysfunction and disruption?

Maple used to feel a sense of honour whenever she looked at the flower. The sacrifices made by her dad and others to protect the country filled her with pride. She would openly talk about it among friends, boasting of her dad's overseas adventures.

Not anymore. These days the sight of the flower filled her with anger and resentment. She felt like the army had taken her dad away from her. Changed him. He wasn't the same dad after he returned from his last tour. He was physically fine but broken inside. She thought the rest of the street looked down on them like a charity case.

Underneath the flower was a doormat which read 'Welcome Home'. Maple thought their house had to be the most unwelcoming in the area. Filled with grief, drama and sadness.

She spat on the lawn. The blades of grass were at least six inches long, a stark contrast to their neighbours, whose lawns were nicely mown, with impressive hedges and flower beds.

She hadn't mown the lawn in months. Couldn't care less. It was a way for her to give the finger to the rest of the street who'd abandoned her, like a thorn in the community's side.

'How've you been, Maple?' a voice called out. It was their neighbour Mrs Pyke, an excessively friendly soul in her eighties, who'd spent most of her adult life in the neighbourhood.

Maple closed her eyes wishing she was somewhere else. The last thing she wanted was to engage in conversation with the old biddy.

She opened her eyes and attempted a smile. 'Yeah, we're okay, Mrs Pyke. Taking it day by day.' She resented small talk with neighbours, regardless of how nice they were. She felt patronised and belittled. She often kept her answers short in an attempt to end the conversations sooner.

Mrs Pyke smiled. Her curly grey hair burst out of her white floppy hat. Maple waited for the day a moth would fly out of her hair. It looked like a large accumulation of dust in a tired wardrobe.

She often struggled to look her in the eye. The hair

on Mrs Pyke's upper lip was dark and visible. She couldn't understand why the old lady wouldn't just wax it off. Surely her friends or family had commented on it. Maybe she just didn't care.

Maple felt guilty for harbouring such awful thoughts. Mrs Pyke had always been a tower of strength for her family, whenever her dad was serving overseas and they needed a helping hand.

Whether it was preparing them a meal or helping with the laundry, Mrs Pyke was one of the most generous people Maple knew.

'Good to hear, sweetie,' Mrs Pyke said. 'You know you're always welcome to drop by my place to have a chat. Doesn't matter what the topic is. I'm all ears. I know how you must feel. When my husband returned from the Korean War many years ago, we had our struggles. They seem to leave in one piece and come back in tatters. It's a strange thing, war.'

'Thanks Mrs Pyke, you're a star. I'll keep that in mind. Anyway, I'd better get to school. Don't want to be late.'

'Of course. Before you go, how's your mum?

Maple bit her bottom lip. She was still furious at her mum but didn't see any point in being honest.

'She's doing a lot better, thanks. Keeping busy as always. You know what she's like.'

'Well, that's good to hear. See you, sweetie. You have a nice day. If you ever need anything, don't hesitate to ask. We need to look after our poppy families.'

Maple walked along the footpath. 'Bloody Mrs Pyke,' she whispered. 'I'd rather drink cleaning detergent than spend more time with you, staring at your moustache.'

The neighbourhood was typical of middle-class suburban Australia – a mixture of modest red brick and weatherboard homes on quarter acre blocks. The warmth of the beginning of summer had brought back the sound of lawn mowers, sprinklers and people beavering away in their gardens.

It was an aspirational community – the families weren't wealthy by any stretch, but they worked hard, often in jobs they didn't enjoy, just to pay the bills and ensure their children experienced a decent upbringing.

Not all homes were the same. Some took more pride in their appearance and maintenance than others. Those with impressive and elaborate gardens frowned on those who left their gardens bare and whose windows were covered in cobwebs.

A family's front lawn and entrance was almost like an alter ego for those living on the street. You could tell a lot about someone's character and personality by looking at their front yard.

Those with manicured lawns and blossoming flowers considered themselves a cut above the rest – successful and hardworking, mindful of what others thought about them; while those whose front yards had seen better days took a more carefree approach to life – undeterred by the thoughts and opinions of others.

Few people looked her in the eye as she walked past. Maple felt more like a stranger these days since her dad left. Before that day, people would always say hi and ask how she was doing. Other than Mrs Pyke, it seemed like the rest of the street avoided her like the plague.

Like the rest of suburban Australian, the neighbourhood was filled with hypocrisy and secrecy, which irritated Maple. There were so-called happily married couples who routinely cheated on each other; wives who were used as boxing bags by their husbands and drug addict kids.

Men and women who initially opposed a large supermarket chain setting up shop in the community now worked there. It made her sick. No one seemed to have any sense of conviction.

Yet, despite this melting pot of social decay, these families carried on as if everything was normal – nothing to see here.

Image meant everything to them. It may not have been the fanciest street but keeping face and purporting to lead a life of respectability was important.

Maple reached into her right skirt pocket and retrieved a scrunched-up photo. It was about five years old, and she took it wherever she went.

She looked at the crinkly colour picture. Her dad stood alongside her, his arm wrapped around her shoulder as she held a soccer trophy for being best and fairest player that season. Their faces beamed with smiles. He was clean-shaven. Maple remembered him telling her he never trusted a man with a beard – it's easier to disguise your emotions and feelings underneath all the fluff.

She had grass stains on her shorts, her shirt had streaks of dirt, while her face dripped with sweat.

It was one of the happiest days in her short life. Her dad attended all her games, always cheering from the sidelines. She looked up to him. He wasn't just her dad, he was her trainer, mentor and biggest fan. She knew she could achieve any goal with his support.

Some days she snuck into her mum's room and went through his old possessions, including his army uniform. Even just for a short while it reminded her of her dad.

She was angry with her dad now, but that photo

brought back good memories, of a better time.

Her stomach grumbled from hunger. She hadn't eaten in more than 12 hours. She kissed the photo and put it back in her pocket.

She passed a familiar house and saw the Schwarz family pile into an SUV – mum, dad and the three kids.

Maple had the hots for the eldest son, Jake. He was in the same year and oozed with charm and sophistication – fit, tanned, intelligent and funny. He always smiled at her when they crossed paths at school.

Only problem was he already had a girlfriend named Cindy. Maple hated her. She had one of those condescending smiles and gossiped non-stop behind people's backs. They'd never gotten along. Always sledged each other.

It all started two years ago during soccer training. They were in the same team. Cindy dribbled the ball towards the posts, when Maple dived in attempting to intercept it. It didn't go to plan.

Maple accidentally took Cindy out, causing her to fall awkwardly and break her ankle. Cindy ended up watching the majority of the season from the sidelines.

Cindy blamed it on Maple, saying she did it on purpose to get her off the team.

Despite Maple's attempted apologies, Cindy never forgave her.

It took Maple about ten minutes to reach Burger Boss, a local fast-food restaurant. It was either that or the local chicken or pizza shop. She'd had enough chicken recently and the owner of the pizza shop could talk underwater and was obsessed with soccer. Whenever she visited, he'd rattle on about the latest A-League news and scores. She used to enjoy such conversations, but she preferred to eat less pizza these days.

It was a cheap-looking place. Hadn't been renovated in years and desperately needed a new lick of paint. Blue leather booths were on both sides, with laminated menus standing in the middle of each table.

She walked towards the counter which was attended by unenthusiastic looking staff. She looked at the large menu displayed above.

It was a long list of the unhealthiest meals you could buy — cheeseburger with fries, bacon and egg burger with wedges, ribs with coleslaw, and chicken nuggets with 'special sauce' — a heart attack for $9.95.

The community wasn't renowned for trendy and fancy establishments. Cheap rent came with cheap tenants. A constant reminder of the class struggle lived day in, day out.

Maple cast her eyes over the guilty pleasures. She used to be on a strict, predominantly vegetarian diet because of her training. The new Maple frowned upon establishments like this—frequented by lazy, overweight no-hopers. Conga lines of obese under-achieving folk lining up to get their weekly dose of excess calories and heart disease. They were the definition of bludgers.

Despite this she didn't mind frequenting such restaurants – for a brief moment it reminded her that some people's lives must be more miserable than hers.

A young girl walked up beside her and scanned the menu.

'So many things to choose from, aren't there? Feel a bit guilty ordering ribs for breakfast. What do you reckon?' the girl asked.

Maple stared at the girl curiously. She looked familiar.

The girl was a few inches shorter, younger, had the bluest eyes Maple had ever seen, and wore the same school uniform.

Her short blonde hair was so straight it looked like someone had ironed it.

Maple looked down at her awkwardly, wondering who this person must be. 'Yeah, guess so. Depends what you fancy at this hour.'

The girl smiled at Maple. The way she looked at Maple was similar to the way kids look at their idols–

beaming with joy and adulation.

'I've tried the ribs before and they're awesome, but way too filling for breakfast,' she said. 'I'd have to skip lunch if I ate those, which I don't want to do because Mum packed me a big lunch today. Might just go with the nuggets then.'

Maple was unimpressed and not in the mood for small talk. 'Then go the nuggets kid. Don't let me get in your way.'

Maple looked down at the girl's scuffed shoes, which looked like they'd been on the receiving end of a few soccer balls.

The girl looked at her scuffed shoes and giggled. 'I can't help myself. Whether it's in the schoolyard or the pitch, I just love playing the game. I'd love to be a Matilda one day. Wouldn't you?'

Maple rolled her eyes and scratched the back of her head. 'I don't know. I suppose so.'

'I've seen you around school,' the girl said. 'You're Maple, right? The awesome soccer player. I like soccer as well, as you can probably tell from these shoes.'

'Yeah, that's me,' she replied bluntly. 'Do you want an autograph or something?'

'No, don't be silly,' the girl replied, slightly taken aback by Maple's dismissive attitude. 'I just think it would be such an incredible life—paid big bucks, travelling around the world first class, adored by fans.'

She pointed at Maple's hands. 'I love your nails, they're so different. Why do you paint them different colours?'

'I just like the colours, that's all. Nothing special.' Maple looked into her blue eyes. She could see a part of her younger self in the girl. Overly enthusiastic, energetic and ever smiling.

'Fair enough. I like it. My name is Vicky. I'm in Year 7. I just think you're pretty awesome that's all. I hear from coaches you could go pro one day. How cool would that be? Why did you stop playing? You're so talented.'

Maple stood still like a statue, her heart racing. She knew the girl.

It was the daughter of her dad's army friend. Their families spent a lot of time together years ago when they were both much younger.

Her mind flooded with memories of the past. Happier times.

Maple reminisced about a trip to the beach in which she helped Vicky build a sandcastle. The happiness and joy it brought both of them was etched in her mind.

'Are you okay?' Vicky asked, confused with Maple's appearance.

Maple shook her head repeatedly, embarrassed

and worried about looking vulnerable.

'What would you know, you little one?' Maple asked aggressively. 'What is some Year 7 kid doing talking to me? Who do you think you are? Are you following me around?'

Vicky started to shake. Tears filled her eyes. 'Sorry, I didn't mean to annoy you. I didn't mean to. It won't happen again. Have a nice day,' she said, before running back towards the entrance.

'Wait, Vicky …' Maple pleaded, regretting her earlier comments and behaviour.

It was too late. Vicky had left the restaurant and bolted, without looking back.

Maple stood still and confused. 'What have I done?' she whispered.

The old Maple would have loved the attention, being looked up to and treated like a celebrity by a kid. The new Maple hated it. Wanted to be left alone and just blend in with the rest of the crowd.

She ordered the cheeseburger with fries and sat alone at a booth. The other booths were occupied by groups of people. People with friends.

As she chewed, she thought about Vicky. Maybe she'd been too hard on the girl. She recalled how difficult Year 7 had been for her. Perhaps she should have been more empathetic and friendly.

She peered out the window. The sun was out but she didn't feel joyous. She wanted the day to be over even though it was only the beginning.

'What is wrong with me?' she asked herself. She continued chewing her meal, every mouthful filled with guilt.

Over the past year she'd transformed into a solitary monster. Despite always being taught to conquer her fears and overcome adversity, she was now someone who quit and gave up easily, frequently at war with life and the people who cared about her.

As she gazed out the window, she saw a father with two children in a playground. They looked so happy, playing on the swings. She remembered being on those same swings as a child, with her parents taking it in turns to push her.

Maple longed to see her dad again. Or even just receive a letter from him. Anything that proved he was alive and well.

She was sick and tired of lying to people about his situation. Whenever someone asked about his welfare, she felt obliged to make something up like he's doing a road trip around the country with some army mates or working interstate, to avoid awkwardness.

She refused to tell the truth. No one could relate to her. She was an outsider. She didn't know anyone else at school with a similar story.

She was all alone.

A group of girls from her school left a nearby booth and headed for the door.

'See you at school, Major Maple,' one of the girls said, causing the rest of the group to laugh.

Maple clenched her firsts.

It was time to go to school. It was the last place she wanted to be.

CHAPTER 3

Mo stepped off the bus with a body board wrapped under his arms and headed towards the school gates. He tucked his white shirt into his grey pants and adjusted his tie, to avoid being told off by teachers.

He'd already spent an afternoon last week in detention and had been grounded by his mum for a week.

He could see teachers parking their vehicles in the carpark. He felt sorry for them as they emerged from their second hand, cheap vehicles and charity shop looking clothes. People should take pride in their appearance.

He walked with a relaxed, confident style, like an Olympic sprinter before a race, headphones on, and his backpack slung across his right shoulder.

He felt like he had the right to strut around like the big man on campus. He'd scored a century for the school's first XI cricket team over the weekend and won them the match. He'd been named man of the match. Not bad for a sixteen-year-old playing up a grade and punching well above his weight.

His teammates and coach treated him like a hero

after the match. He'd never received such adulation in his life, and he loved it.

His black hair was wavy and had only been brushed by his fingers that morning before making a bolt for the bus.

He scratched his face. The black stubble was getting longer and thicker each day. He'd read somewhere that girls prefer guys with facial hair – made them look wiser and more sophisticated. Plus, his favourite cricketer had a beard and a smoking hot girlfriend. He'd never had a girlfriend but wanted one.

Truth be told his face looked like bum fluff. His mum hated it. She thought he looked homeless. Her once handsome son's face resembled that of a wild animal. She didn't move them to the other side of the world so they could be looked down on. She even left a razor and shaving cream next to the bathroom sink each morning as a friendly reminder.

Mo didn't care. Social media sites and influencers were his source of knowledge and truth, not his mum. He spent most evenings in bed, scrolling through images of his idols on his phone. They seemed to have it all – wealth, power and women.

He'd made a bet with his mum – if he achieved at least four As on his report card then he could keep the beard. If he missed out, then it would get the chop.

Fortunately for him he got five As and got to continue wearing his bum fluff with pride.

All his other mates had girlfriends and he thought he was missing out. They proudly showed off their hickeys on their necks at the start of every week, back slapping each other, carrying on like Hollywood stars.

He grew the facial hair in part to annoy his mum – a sort of rebellion against her. She was master and commander of their household and this was a subtle way of showing his independence.

Walking through the gates brought Mo a sense of joy and exhilaration. He liked school. A place where he was an equal and a factory for dreams. He'd be judged on his hard work and attitude, not his ethnicity or religion.

The polar opposite to his past life, where bombs and bullets were often a daily reality.

The kids in the school quadrangle resembled animal groups segregated in their own patch of the savannah. The food chain applied in the schoolyard as well.

Towards the left there were the lions – young men and women who thought they were the coolest kids in school and top of the food chain. Talented, mostly arrogant, self-entitled athletes, whose prowess on the sporting field made them feel superior and above the rest.

To the right you had the zebras – creative, arty kids, who excelled at music, drama and visual arts. Despite their talents, being creative wasn't as cool as being sporty.

Straight ahead were the gazelles – school nerds, who dominated the classrooms and academia. They were often targeted and bullied by the lions for their timidness and physical limitations.

Then there were the giraffes – a bunch of awkward kids. Pretty average at most things, who struggled to fit in with the rest of the crowd.

Mo strutted towards the left and joined his fellow lions.

'Here comes the future opening batsman for the Aussie cricket team,' his teammate Dale said, as Mo approached the group.

'It seriously looks like someone has shaved your arse and put the hair on your face,' Dale said, pointing at Mo's face.

The group burst out laughing. Mo stood there, shaking his head.

'At least I can grow one,' he said. 'Take a look at yourself in the mirror before you judge me, buddy. Your hair is longer than most of the girls in this school. Must be the effeminate side of you coming out.'

Dale was lean with long, curly blonde hair. He

looked like he belonged on a beach with a surfboard tucked under his arms.

Dale began to bow repeatedly in front of him. 'All hail King Mo, all hail King Mo,' he chanted. 'Make sure you get his autograph now before he becomes famous. We'll never see him again.'

The girls chuckled amongst themselves. One of them winked at Mo.

'Cut it out man, it was just one game. No need for the special treatment. Your slingshot right arm helped as well,' Mo replied.

Dale smirked and put his right arm around Mo's shoulders. 'Just one game. You must be kidding. Winning that game, or should I say you winning the game, means we're a step closer to being school association champions. We've never won a championship. We'd be making history. Just imagine seeing your mug in the paper.'

Deep down, Mo welcomed the attention. Growing up, he'd always felt like a shadow, not there in substance, lacking identity and being insignificant.

Since coming to Warrior Beach High School, he'd found friends and purpose, not to mention popularity. A far cry from his old life in another universe. Almost everyone knew of him.

Not just because of his athletic skills, but his brains

too. He'd been Dux of his year the last two years. Teachers raved about him. The school was a humble public school, but they thought Mo had the potential to achieve top marks and make them stand out from the rest. Put their average school on the map.

He did dream of playing cricket for Australia one day, scoring a ton at the Sydney Cricket Ground in front of tens of thousands of fans, being worshipped by kids and paid obscene amounts of money.

'Yeah, hopefully we can get that trophy,' he said, grinning. 'One game at a time, mate.'

'You might even be able to score yourself a girlfriend if we win it,' Dale said.

The group laughed. Mo's heart began to beat a bit faster due to the nerves. He hated being singled out like that.

He replied with a self-deprecating laugh of his own.

'Few more wins and you could have yourself one of these.' Dale pulled his collar down and revealed his latest prized possession—a large, round, red hickey shone brightly on his neck. It was the size of a ping-pong ball and looked new.

Dale winked at Kristy, who was standing a few metres away. 'Courtesy of Saturday's party at Mick's. Kristy was all over me like a rash. You missed the show, being grounded.'

'You must be quite the charmer, mate,' Mo said.

Dale patted Mo on the back. 'You could learn a lot from me, mate. You might be the one scoring on the field, but I'm the one scoring off it.'

'Get over yourself,' interrupted a girl. It was Kristy, Dale's on and off again girlfriend. She had shoulder length dark brown hair and wore pink lipstick. The type of girl who spends way too much time trying to be a social media influencer. She tried to cover her acne up with make-up.

Her skirt was above the knees, and it was widely known she inflated her chest by stuffing tissues down her bra. She thought she was the hottest girl in school.

'You think you're some kind of hotshot. You just got lucky. Good thing for you I'd had a few to drink.'

Dale shook his head and smiled. 'Oh, give me a break, babe. You were begging for it all night. You snogged my neck like it was your last meal.'

'You're a loser,' Kristy said, pushing Dale in the chest. 'You're such a liar. I agree with Mo, it's time for a haircut. It's longer than mine.'

Kristy turned to face Mo. 'Don't listen to him. He adds no value,' she said, before walking away with two girlfriends.

Dale looked Mo in the eyes and chuckled. 'Sometimes I wish I was like you, man.'

'What's that supposed to mean?' queried Mo.

'Come on man, you're sixteen-years-old and you've never dated a girl, let alone kissed one.'

'That's not true. How would you know, anyway?'

'Well, prove me wrong then.'

'Kristy was right, you are a loser, man,' Mo snapped.

'Hey, I'm just telling you the truth. A good friend tells you what you should hear, not what you want to hear. I'm doing you a favour.'

'What about that Maple girl? You guys share history class together, don't you?'

'Yeah, so what?' asked Mo.

'She's cute and sporty. Why don't you ask her out?'

'She seems cool, but a bit of a loner these days,' Mo replied.

'Takes one to know one,' Dale said, laughing. 'What are you doing with that body board, mate? As if you can swim, let alone use that thing.'

Mo rolled his eyes, but deep down he knew it was a fair question. He hadn't body boarded since he was in primary school.

'Yeah, real funny, mate. How long do you think I've been in this country? Our school has the word beach in it. It's in our DNA. I know what I'm doing.'

'Yeah right. Don't forget to swim between the flags. And remember this important point – make sure you tie the strap on your ankle. It makes a huge difference.'

'Yep, got it, mate.' Mo made a note of the advice in his head.

The school bell rang. First class started in five minutes. The school's animal kingdom dispersed in every direction, with lions barging their way past gazelles and zebras.

For students like Dale and Kristy it was the start of the daily grind. Neither were academically inclined nor overly ambitious.

Dale talked about going to university but knew he'd probably end up doing a trade apprenticeship like his older brother.

Mo had helped him out with assignments on more than one occasion.

Dale and Kristy preferred the social aspect of school life.

They shared an unfortunate bond – both were from broken families. Dale hadn't seen his mum in years, while Kristy's dad walked out on the family three years ago. They acted tough and resilient but hurt inside. It was like a part of their hearts had been stripped away.

Mo knew something was wrong. Despite being mates, he rarely visited Dale's home. He never asked him about his family life. Didn't have the nerve.

Dale took a deep breath. 'Come along then, mate,

another day in Warrior Beach Prison.'

'Yeah, all we need is some barbed wire along the fences and it would be prison. Don't worry, couple more years and you'll be released,' Mo said.

'Can't wait.'

Mo charged off to his first class – history. The bell was the sound of opportunity and potential. There's a good chance he wouldn't have even gone to school back in his old country, let alone be Dux or a star cricketer.

His life would probably have been defined by hardship, poverty and violence. He didn't take anything for granted.

His mum always reminded him of how fortunate they were to have a new start in life. Opportunities couldn't be wasted.

He walked down the hallway of the Humanities building. History was his favourite subject.

Learning about ancient and modern conflicts and past civilizations gave him a different perspective. People and cultures he could relate to. He didn't feel like an outsider when he read those books.

The old building was in need of some love and renovation – the paint was peeling and some of the notices on the noticeboard were so ancient and faded they looked like they'd been pinned up by a former generation of students.

It seemed unbefitting and somewhat ironic to be taught about some of the greatest leaders who have ever lived in a building that looked like it was about to fall apart, in a school with the word warrior in it.

As he approached the classroom, a deep voice called out.

'Mo, can I speak to you for one minute, please?'

Mo stopped, closed his eyes and groaned. He recognised the voice. It was Mr Fredericks, the school counsellor. He was overweight, but by the way he dressed, seemed to be unaware.

His bulging stomach hung over his worn belt, while the buttons on his shirt that was a size too small, looked like they were about to burst off.

He drove a tired, embarrassing looking Ford hatchback that hadn't been washed in months. The epitome of hopeless. Why should anyone take advice, especially emotional advice from such a dour looking human being?

Mo didn't know whether to feel sorrier for Mr Fredericks or his belt. Hopefully someone in his family would be kind enough to gift him a new one for Christmas.

Mo turned to face the man and forced a smile. 'Sure thing, Mr Fredericks. How can I help?'

Mr Fredericks coughed into his hands. Mo could smell the tobacco on him.

He was a pack a day smoker who spent half the day standing outside the school gates puffing cancer sticks.

He cleared his throat before speaking. 'Look, I've put together a new mentoring group that meets during lunchtime. It pairs mature, hardworking students like yourself with younger kids who need a bit of inspiring. They're good kids with good hearts, but I worry they need someone to look up to.'

He paused and coughed again. 'I think you'd be a good fit for this new group. If you agree, then I'd like you to attend the first meeting which starts today. I think the kids would enjoy meeting you. You and your mother have obviously seen your fair share of challenges in life. Hearing from you could give them a new perspective on life.'

Mo looked him in the eyes and smiled. Inside he was thinking this sounded like the most boring way to spend a lunchtime, especially in a meeting coordinated by the most uninspiring man in school, who would probably spend most of the time smoking outside.

He also hated being labelled like that. Teachers and staff always made assumptions about him because of where he'd come from. Boy from a war-torn country.

The despair and struggles he must have endured.

What would Mr Fredericks know? He probably spent more time eating burgers and chips than learning about different cultures.

'Sure, glad to, sir, happy to help if you think I can be of assistance,' Mo said, reluctantly.

Not that he had much choice.

Mr Fredericks grinned. 'Wonderful. We'll see you at 12.30pm in room 12B in this building then. Look forward to it.'

Mo turned back around and entered the classroom. Rows of single wooden desks lined the room. He sat down in the middle row surrounded by twenty others.

The fan blades hummed above his head. He looked up at them. Their furious spinning action reminded him of helicopters back in his old home. Their sight and sound brought him a mixture of emotions – a sense of calmness that everything would be okay, coupled with violence and bloodshed.

He closed his eyes and took a deep breath.

Sitting to Mo's right was Lexi – a bubble gum chewing girl with attitude. She sat there doodling pictures of dogs on her desk. Her black hair was shaven on the sides and shorter than most of the guys in school. The first few buttons on her top were undone, showing off parts of her pink bra. Her face was overshadowed by her mascara-ringed eyes.

Lexi spent more time in detention than anyone else and was a teacher's worst nightmare – regularly interrupting class, picking on other students and submitting assignments late. Her most recent triumph was calling in a bomb hoax to delay a maths exam.

Mo could never understand why someone would choose to be so troublesome. What did she have to gain from engaging in anti-social behaviour? Why did she sport such a boyish, military-style hair cut?

Sitting to Mo's left was Travis – an academically gifted student who dominated debating and chess. He was shorter than the average sixteen-year-old and had curly red hair. His trousers were about an inch shorter than they should be, so you could always see his socks when he walked. His shirt was tucked into his blue underwear and his tie was also awkwardly short– about belly button length. An archetypal geek.

Classmates often referred to him as ginger pubes – a few years earlier when competing in the annual swimming carnival, he'd forgotten to tighten his one size too big budgie smugglers before diving in, causing them to slip down in front of the crowd, exposing the crown jewels. Clearly time doesn't heal all wounds.

They'd studied together a few times. Mo considered him a good bloke but wouldn't dare associate with him for fear of being ridiculed and ostracised by his mates.

They'd never forgive him. Lions don't hang out with gazelles. The food chain didn't work like that.

Sitting behind the gazelle was Max–a softly spoken Korean Australian kid. He was closeted, but that didn't stop the likes of Dale calling him a faggot and teasing him.

Their school wasn't exactly the most progressive institution.

Max never fought back from any of the abuse and just copped it on the chin. His older friends who had come out told him to persevere–there's a light at the end of the tunnel they always said. Couple more years and he could finally be himself.

Mo's heart began to beat a bit faster when the girl he fancied entered the room.

She swanned on in like she had no care in the world, with an expressionless look on her face. She was slim and had shoulder length black hair.

Her fingernails caught his attention. The mixture of black and green polish was a contrast to the glitzy, princess types with whom he usually associated.

She plonked her books on top of the desk in front of him and sat down, without even so much as a glance at Mo.

The girl then leaned forward and placed her head

in her arms, as if she was about to fall asleep.

Mo wondered if something was wrong with her. Had she not slept the night before? Was something bothering her? He didn't have the courage to ask.

Before he could ponder any further, the teacher walked into the room – Mr Dryparsons.

He wasn't exactly a male model – dressed in beige trousers, an ivory-coloured shirt that looked like he'd inherited from his grandfather, with brown leather shoes in desperate need of a polish. His most distinguishing facial feature was his eyebrows–so bushy and complex, no one would be surprised if a moth flew out. This was coupled with his brown moustache, which looked better suited to the 1970s.

He was bald and his height, or lack thereof, ironically stood out. Some kids referred to him as the school garden gnome.

He didn't wear a tie, despite the top button on his shirt being done up. Mo thought this looked peculiar. Was he hiding something? Surely he didn't get a hickey over the weekend.

He drove a pathetic looking third hand Suzuki hatchback.

Despite these shortcomings, Mo had a level of respect for him. He taught with a rigour and passion that had been foreign to him.

Mr Dryparsons placed his notepad and textbook on his bigger desk at the front of the room and wrote on the whiteboard.

He wrote the words 'MODERN CONFLICTS' in large letters, before putting the marker down and turning to face his class.

'Okay folks, eyes on me. Today we're focusing on the important topic of modern conflicts. Can anyone please help explain what a modern conflict is exactly?'

Mr Dryparsons scoured the room, looking for eager hands to rise.

The only student who raised their hand was Travis. His right arm was so stretched, it looked like he could tear a muscle.

'Yes, Travis,' Mr Dryparsons said reluctantly, hoping someone else would answer the question.

'Well, that depends on your definition of modern sir,' Travis said audaciously. 'Some define modern as being post the Second World War, while others believe it to be even earlier than that, dating back to the beginning of the twentieth century.'

Lexi rolled her eyes and mimed 'complete loser' to herself.

'What was that?' Mr Dryparsons asked, catching her inaudible remark.

Lexi folded her arms. 'Nothing sir, I was just yawning.'

'Perhaps you should try to get more sleep then.'

Mr Dryparsons turned to face Travis. 'That's correct, Travis. The period is up for debate. For the purposes of today's discussion, let's focus on the post Second World War period. Who can tell me Australia's longest ever war?'

Travis's right arm shot up again.

Mr Dryparsons looked around the room. He took a few steps forward and looked down at the female student sitting in front of Mo, who looked asleep, with her head resting against her arms on the desk.

'Time to wake up, Maple,' he said, raising his voice.

Maple's shoulders shook in shock as she raised her head in surprise.

'Any ideas, Maple?'

'Sorry, what was the question again?' she asked, yawning.

The class burst out laughing.

Mr Dryparsons shook his head and folded his arms in frustration.

'I was asking if you knew which conflict was Australia's longest war?'

'No idea,' she grunted.

The class continued laughing.

'Why don't you have a guess then?' he insisted. His eyes widened in anger with every word. Some hairs on his moustache moved as he breathed heavily through his nostrils.

Maple ran her fingers through her black hair and rotated her head from side to side. Being stuck in class with the most unattractive and boring man in the universe didn't interest her. Neither did learning about some stupid war that meant nothing to her.

'The Ashes,' she said.

'The Ashes?' Mr Dryparsons asked curiously.

'Yes, the cricket war between Australia and England. The war continues this summer on our own turf.'

Mr Dryparsons ground his teeth and started picking at a fingernail.

'You think this is funny, do you?'

'Not really, I never said I'm a comedian. Does it really matter?'

'Does what really matter?'

'Our longest war. I mean who really gives a damn? I'm sure it will be surpassed by another pointless war in the future.'

Mr Dryparsons' face turned red with rage.

'That's it, get out!' he yelled. 'Go straight to the school counsellor's office. I've had enough of you and your attitude. You used to be one of my top students. I won't have you waste our time and be rude.'

'Don't mind if I do,' Maple said. She stood up, gathered her belongings and stormed out of the room.

Mo looked on with astonishment. He liked people with a sense of humour. Plus, it sounded like she enjoys cricket. Good looks plus a cricket fan. Win-win.

Mr Dryparsons turned his attention to him.

'Mo, what do you reckon? Our longest war that is? I'm sure you'd know.'

Mo despised being pigeonholed. Sometimes he felt like his brown skin put a target on his back. Like he spoke on behalf of all people with his background.

'Yes sir, I have a good idea of what the answer is,' he replied, secretly longing to learn more about Maple instead.

CHAPTER 4

The school bell rang loud and clear. The clock in the classroom read 12.30pm. Lunchtime.

Students bolted towards the door. The animal kingdom united in their desire to enjoy their daily feed. Some gazelles got pushed and shoved by lions on the way out.

The sound of the bell ringing ordinarily would be met with excitement and joy from Mo as he could hang out with his mates for forty-five minutes. A break from the daily grind and a chance to discuss the latest gossip. Who was now dating who? Who'd recently made out in the toilets?

Today it meant mentoring some annoying kids who had nothing better to do than waste his precious lunchtime. The definition of boredom. What would he say to them? What is mentoring anyway?

Mo wrestled his way past his English class and walked towards room 12B with a grimace on his face.

He didn't even bother acknowledging Dale and Kristy, whose tongues must have been so far down each other's throats they could feel their tonsils, whilst leaning against a set of lockers. Not even a tornado could stop those two going at it.

Dale opened his eyes as Mo approached and winked, before closing them again.

Mo shook his head and whispered 'lucky bastard' to himself. Why is it the biggest morons always get the most action?

He arrived at the room a few minutes later.

The letter B on the door was on its last legs–symbolic of the entire school, which seemed to be a shadow of its former self.

He strolled into the room with that athletic swagger, took one look at the anxious looking kids sitting at the front and made his way to a desk at the back. The kids looked like a future bunch of giraffes and zebras.

He undid the top of his tie and applied spray on deodorant underneath his armpits. He sprayed so much the smell consumed the entire room.

He wanted to look relaxed and tough in front of them. Mark his territory.

The walls were covered in posters promoting healthy lifestyle – from contraception and safe sex–to warnings about the dangers of drug use.

The school had a mixed bag of anti-social behaviour. It was commonplace for there to be at least one teen pregnancy each year. Mo and his mates would place bets on who it would be next.

Six months ago, a Year 11 girl named Belle was the one with the bun in the oven. She made up some lie that she was switching schools.

She'd been spotted at the local shopping centre last week struggling to comfort a screaming child. Dale had guessed correctly and scored himself a six pack.

Mo reached into his backpack and retrieved a sandwich wrapped in plastic. He undid the wrapping and took a bite. It was cheese, tomato and egg. His favourite. His mates always bagged him out for eating the same thing every day, but he didn't care. When you've found something good you stick to it.

Six Year 7 kids sat at the front. They looked nervous but eager – constantly fidgeting, between mouthfuls of whatever their mums had made them for lunch.

Their small stature and high-pitched voices projected a sense of innocence. No life responsibilities. Report cards didn't matter. They could just enjoy life.

A couple of them turned around and smiled at Mo, but after seeing the unwelcome look on his face, quickly turned back around. You don't disturb a lion while it's eating, otherwise you risk becoming prey.

Four more Year 10 student mentors entered the classroom and sat near Mo. They looked as enthusiastic as he did – their faces wore sombre expressions as if they were about to visit a dentist.

Mo leaned back on his chair and gazed at the ceiling. *What did I do to deserve this? Why me?*

He was about to pack up his things and leave for greener pastures, when Maple entered the room.

His heart raced again.

She walked towards him. Mo stopped chewing and just stared at her.

'Can we sit anywhere, or do we have specific spots to sit?' she asked.

Mo chewed and swallowed his food. 'Anywhere,' he replied.

Maple sat next to him. The most boring lunchtime imaginable now just got a bit more interesting for Mo. She looked around the classroom and spotted a familiar face a few metres away. It was Vicky.

Maple still felt terrible for her behaviour earlier and wanted to apologise. She smiled at Vicky when their eyes met.

Vicky looked down at her desk, pretending to write on a notepad. Maple was the last person she wanted to speak to.

Maple turned to face Mo. 'So, I suppose you got roped into this by Fredericks as well then?' she asked, half smiling.

Mo felt more nervous now than he did when batting in a big cricket match. The girl who appeared in some of his dreams was not only sitting next to him, but talking to him as well.

'Sure did. Sounds stupid and a waste of time.'

Maple shrugged her shoulders. 'I didn't exactly have much of a choice. The counsellor said I could either attend this session or attend detention. I didn't want to waste my afternoon in detention, so I chose the lesser of two evils.'

Mo found her raw and refreshing. A sharp contrast to the many straight-laced kids out there.

'I would have made the same decision as you.'

Maple looked at him with a confused look on her face. 'I thought you just said it sounded stupid?

'Well, I um, yeah. Let's see. Could be fun, but could be stupid at the same time.'

'Right. That makes a lot of sense.'

Mo wished he could sink into his chair and disappear after seeing the confused look on her face. His stomach dropped.

How does Dale do it? Why I am I so bad at talking to girls? he wondered.

Seeing Mr Fredericks walk into the room brought Mo a sense of relief and distraction. He'd never been happier to see the school counsellor and his 1970s moustache.

Mr Fredericks took one look at the scattered class and shook his head.

'Okay folks, this set up isn't going to work. Mentoring is about engagement, not separation. What we're going to do is put you all in pairs. Now there's six Year 7 students and six Year 10 students. Do the math. Let's go.'

He clicked his fingers in the air.

The students jumped from their seats and zigged in and out of each other like a herd of cattle. Mo stood still, admiring the odd spectacle. Without any direction, students began to pair with each other. It seemed almost natural.

Within a minute, everyone was paired except for him and a young girl, who stood nervously, hands behind her back, looking at the ground.

Mo walked towards the girl. 'I guess we're a pair.'

The girl looked up, smiling. 'Yeah, sounds good. You're that awesome cricketer, aren't you? I'm Vicky,' she said, holding out her hand.

Mo shook her hand, surprised at the girl's formality. 'Nice to meet you. Yeah, that's me. I'm Mo.'

The pair sat down at a desk, facing each other.

'Mo?' Vicky asked curiously. 'Like moustache?'

Mo grinned. 'No, it's short for Mohammed. I get that a lot. I figured everything else in this country gets abbreviated, so I may as well abbreviate my name as well.'

'Cool. I like that. Way cooler than my name.'

'What's Vicky short for?' asked Mo.

'Victoria,' she said, laughing. 'I don't know what my parents were thinking, naming me after a state. Especially one we've never lived in.'

'At least it's a nice state. Could be worse,' Mo said. 'At least they didn't name you Tassie.'

Mr Fredericks interrupted them, clapping his hands and climbed on top of a desk in the middle of the room. It was a contradictory sight — a garden gnome towering over the class. The group looked on in bewilderment.

'Okay folks, looks like you've all paired up. That's the hard bit done. Welcome to the inaugural Warrior Beach Mentoring Workshop. I look forward to this being the first of many.'

Mo rolled his eyes and bit his tongue. He thought today was a one-off, not part of a program. This was torturous. What had he signed up for?

Mr Fredericks continued. 'What I want you to all concentrate on today is getting to know one another. Despite your age differences, I think you'll realise you have more in common than you might think. Learn a bit more about each other's backgrounds and their stories. I'll stop talking now. Ask away.'

He then jumped off the desk and sat in a corner of

the room, like a gnome hiding away in its garden bed.

Vicky stared at Mo, who was gazing at the clock. At least another half hour of this madness.

The other pairs were busy, beavering away in deep conversation.

Mo turned to face her. Vicky was a good six inches shorter than him, and her long blonde hair and blue eyes contrasted sharply with his mop like black hair and dark brown eyes.

He felt sorry for that soft white skin of hers–puberty would be tough, with big red pimples contrasting against it.

Her uniform was well-ironed and worn perfectly. Typical nerdy Year 7 kid.

'So where should we start?' asked Mo.

'I can if you like,' Vicky said.

'Go for it then.'

'Sure. Where do I start? You know my name is Vicky. I'm in Year 7. I love soccer. My surname is Jacobs. I …'

'Hold fire,' Mo said, interrupting her. Vicky sat motionless.

'How did you become a part of this program anyway? Did you volunteer or were you forced to do it?'

'Mr Fredericks spoke to me about it last week. He thought I could benefit from it.'

A puzzled look covered Mo's face. 'So, you enjoy wasting your lunchtime? Don't you have friends?' he asked aggressively.

Vicky fidgeted nervously, looking uneasy, as if surrounded by a pack of wild animals.

'No … I just thought it would be a bit of fun that's all. Mr Fredericks said he was recruiting some inspiring Year 10 kids to talk to us. When I bumped into him an hour ago, he said you'd joined the program and I got really excited.'

'Why is that?' asked Mo.

'You have it all. You're smart, popular and good at sport. I want to know your secret. People look up to you.'

Mo felt a bit guilty for being intimidating. The girl clearly looked up to him. He'd need to get used to the attention if he was going to be a pro cricketer some day.

He scratched the bum fluff on his face and looked at Vicky like an adoring fan. 'Fair enough. Sorry for interrupting. Let me hear more about you.'

Vicky smiled and began to relax. 'I'm the middle child in my family. I have an older sister and a younger brother. Do you have siblings?'

'No, I'm an only child. So what do your parents do?'

Vicky looked at the desk and paused before replying. 'Mum works at a local grocery store. It's just me, Mum and my siblings now. My dad passed away a while ago.'

Mo felt bad for asking the question. He could tell it was difficult for her to talk about. Vicky looked like she was using every ounce of energy to hold back tears.

'You're not alone,' he said, attempting to cheer her up.

Vicky looked up.

'What do you mean?'

'My dad passed away a long time ago as well. It's just my mum and me at home.'

Vicky was stunned. Not only was one of her idols sitting opposite her, but he could relate as well.

'I'm so sorry to hear that,' she said.

'Don't worry. It was when I was little and living in a war-torn country.'

'Yeah, I can only imagine how difficult it must have been losing him,' Vicky said. 'My dad died during the Afghanistan War while serving with the army. Not long after we left town and moved around a bit. We only returned to Warrior Beach last year. It's not the same without him. I feel as though I had to grow up a lot and really quickly.

'How so?' asked Mo.

'I help Mum out a lot with cooking, cleaning and assisting my younger brother with his homework.'

Mo felt inspired with what he was hearing.

The pair continued chatting for the remainder of the lunch, almost needing to be dragged out of the room by Mr Fredericks when the bell rang.

CHAPTER 5

Valour tossed around in his red sleeping bag, wide awake. He stared at the afternoon sky. It was clear blue, not a cloud anywhere. The sun shone through the alleyway in Warrior Beach, acting like a wake-up call.

Red was his favourite colour and reminded him of poppy flowers–symbols of war remembrance and commemoration. Respecting the war dead and those still living with the wounds of war. It also reminded him of all the bloodshed from war.

Although these days he felt like the community had forgotten about its veterans.

His back ached from the hard, concrete surface. An old scrunched up newspaper served as his pillow. He'd forgotten what a proper one felt like and couldn't recall the last time he'd slept in a proper bed.

He felt like he deserved to be in pain. A form of punishment and atonement for his sins. The only way he could cope with his inner demons was to be out of his comfort zone day and night. It was as if living a rough and tough life justified his miserable and solitary existence.

He scratched his long, brown beard. It had been months since his last shave. It was so thick and bushy, it looked like a bird's nest. The army would never have allowed such forest-like growth on one of its soldiers. He was taught and trained to be a gentleman–inside and outside.

He certainly didn't look anything like a gentleman now. More like a beast. Someone you'd best avoid.

A small piece of leftover sausage fell from the long, curly fluff dangling from his face.

Before he could even get a glance at yesterday's breakfast, now lying on the ground, a rat bolted from a drainpipe and fled with it.

Valour sat up and closed his eyes, wondering how it had come to this – having to compete with rodents, sleeping in a cold alleyway every night.

'Get a job, you bum!' yelled a man walking by, dressed in a suit. The man's eyes were filled with resentment, like the man in the sleeping bag was inferior. 'You're not helping anyone just sleeping there.'

Valour didn't respond. It made him mad but the last thing he needed was to get into a fight with a stranger. Plus no one would take his word over the other man's. Who would believe a beast over a man in a suit?

He was angered by the man's lack of respect. He looked about the same age as him.

So much for empathy and compassion.

It wasn't that long ago people would shout messages of support and encouragement from the sidelines of military marches, thanking him for his service and bravery.

What a difference a fancy uniform makes.

His thoughts were interrupted by a warm liquid falling on his head, running down his cheeks. His eyes remained shut.

He thought it must be a sun shower. At least the rain would help alleviate the body odour he constantly carried with him.

More liquid continued to drop on his head. He wiped his face and noticed something different about it. It was thicker than rainwater and unusually warm. It also had a foul, awful smell to it.

He opened his eyes and looked down at his hands. It wasn't a sun shower.

'Ahhhhhh!' he screamed, staring at the black and white bird poo, dripping from his fingers.

The stench was overwhelming, and Valour felt like throwing up.

He looked up and saw a magpie circling above. The bird looked relieved, slowly flapping its wings, before flying away.

Valour clenched his fists in anger, grinding his

teeth. How could such a small creature release quite so much poo? he wondered.

He huffed. 'Get out of here, filthy bird!' he said, punching the air in frustration. It was pointless — the culprit had long gone.

He burst out of his sleeping bag and rushed to rinse his face and hands under a nearby tap. He wore army camouflage pants and a black t-shirt. Patched up holes peppered his pants, a daily reminder of his imperfect life.

All the noise and commotion woke Sapper.

His four-legged companion reluctantly stood up, yawned and shook his head, unimpressed with the early start. He enjoyed his afternoon naps.

His tan coloured collar jingled as he walked over to Valour's side, tugging at his leg, his stomach growling from hunger.

'Not now, Sapper,' Valour objected, trying to get all the magpie's droppings off his body. 'Yuck. Worst possible start to the afternoon.'

Sapper grew increasingly impatient. 'Woof!' he barked, before jumping on Valour's chest and licking his neck.

'Alright, alright, you win,' Valour conceded, turning the tap off and patting Sapper on his head. 'Let's get you some food.'

It was busy and the surrounding streets became congested. Men and women, mostly dressed in corporate clothing, hurried past on the main street on their way back to work or a coffee break, ignoring the pair.

Valour tied the laces on his dirty white sneakers — a stark contrast to the shiny black shoes of those walking by. He used to wear similar shiny shoes.

Valour and Sapper walked past a wall with a mural of an Australian Army rising sun symbol above large words which read 'SUPPORT OUR SOLDIERS'.

Valour looked down at Sapper, whose tail was still wagging excitedly in anticipation of his next meal.

'So much for supporting us, hey buddy?' he asked sarcastically. 'Words are just a collection of empty letters without action, mate.'

Unlike most people who have a roof over their heads and a warm soft bed to retire to every night, Valour and Sapper had spent the last few years living on the streets, and sleeping on the cold, unforgiving ground — often having to fend off annoying rodents and revolting creepy crawlies.

A white ibis pecked furiously at something in a nearby rubbish bin. Valour walked over, shooed the bin chicken away and picked up a pizza box from the top.

He opened the box and smiled. There were a few slices left.

'It's still warm,' Valour said in surprise, chewing the pizza.

It was his first meal in twenty-four hours, and he cherished every bite. He didn't have the luxury of guaranteed meals. Every day brought new challenges.

Sapper looked at him with sad puppy dog eyes. He rubbed his back along Valour's legs, begging for a slice.

'You can do better than this, mate,' Valour grumbled, his mouth full of pizza. 'Let's get you something nicer.'

Valour returned to his sleeping bag, packed it up neatly in his army backpack, with a teddy bear protruding from the top.

Valour glanced at a puddle next to his feet, a reminder of last night's rain.

He stared at the puddle like it was a mirror. He adjusted the red headband on his long brown hair and ran his fingers through his overgrown beard.

He was looking nothing like his former self. His once clean-shaven face, short haircut look was now more reminiscent of a caveman than a warrior.

He was unrecognisable. Going from soldier to civilian wasn't a smooth process. Far from it. It was a disaster.

Once a star army recruit and poster boy, he was now the last person the military would want to promote. More like someone they'd prefer to sweep under the carpet.

Since leaving the military, Valour felt alone and lacking purpose. His routine-based days were filled with emptiness and meaningless activities.

Valour looked at Sapper, attempting a smile, before glancing back at the mural on the wall. 'I am the captain of my soul,' he whispered to his four-legged mate, before throwing his backpack on.

'Alright, Sapper, let's see what today's adventure is like,' he said, leaving the alleyway.

The pair walked slowly along the boardwalk, seconds from the beach and its fine, golden sand. Valour towered over everyone – his large stature and height made him stand out from the crowd like a sore thumb.

People of all ages were taking advantage of the pleasant December weather and hitting the water.

The Warrior Beach neighbourhood in New South Wales was famed for its boardwalk–always buzzing with musicians, artists and food trucks.

Few passers-by looked Valour in the eye. They avoided him like the plague, choosing instead to walk around him. This was in stark contrast to Valour's old life when he was with the army–people would often smile and look at him with respect when he used to walk along the same boardwalk in his army uniform, medals hanging from his chest.

Not anymore. Despite being the same person, people now looked down on him, like he was different.

Sapper, on the other hand, was treated like a celebrity, with adults and children alike flocking to pat him and say hello.

As the pair walked further, the sound of light-hearted music grew louder.

'Hey, Valour!' shouted an African Australian man, waving and holding a saxophone.

Valour recognised the voice and looked towards the man. 'Hey, Stevie,' he yelled back, walking towards the man.

He liked Stevie, who was always chilled and treated him with respect.

Stevie was muscular, tall and bald and had a pair of classic aviator sunglasses on. He wore a vintage fedora and a pair of black suspenders over his white shirt and grey dress pants–the polar opposite to Valour. His saxophone case was littered with gold and silver coins.

'I tell you man, every time I see you that hair and beard look longer, like I could make a blanket out of it,' Stevie said cheerfully, putting his saxophone down.

He pointed at a small object protruding from his face. 'Why do you even need a backpack? You could just carry all those things in that hair. What's that in your beard?'

Valour scratched his beard, causing a bit of salami to fall out.

Valour laughed. 'I know, mate, it's a bit wild but at least it keeps me warm during the colder months. Plus, if I shaved it, you wouldn't recognise me anymore.'

He cleared his throat before continuing. 'Have you thought about going up a shirt size? That one looks like it's about to blast off your body.'

Stevie burst out laughing. His entire body joined in, shaking with excitement.

'No point having them if you're not going to show them off,' he said, pointing to his big biceps.

His response reminded Valour of his late mate.

Sapper interrupted the conversation by barking loudly. He was frustrated and starving. Stevie knelt beside him, patting his head.

'Looks to me like the little man needs a feed,' he chuckled, looking up at Valour.

'Yeah, he's starving,' Valour replied, rubbing Sapper's neck. 'Off to find him some nice afternoon tea. After everything he's done for me, he deserves better than some second-hand pizza.'

'Sure does,' Stevie said, winking at Sapper. 'Those stories you told me about him in the Afghanistan War are incredible. He deserves a statue or something.'

Valour nodded. 'Got anything planned today other than playing music?' he asked.

Stevie's eyes widened with delight. 'You bet, my friend. Spending the evening with my daughter. Can't wait to see her. What about you, do you have family plans?'

'What do you mean?' asked Valour, scratching the back of his head, unsure of the question.

'The school holidays are coming up man,' replied Stevie, looking confused. 'You get to relax, eat heaps and spend more time with family.'

Valour looked down at the ground awkwardly, fidgeting his fingers. His heart began to race. He felt like disappearing. He had no idea it was holiday season. He'd lost count of the last time he'd seen his family.

'No, mate, it's just Sapper and me,' he replied eventually, his face turning red from embarrassment.

Stevie could sense something was wrong and that it was a tough conversation for him. 'Oh, all good man. It's such a nice day. I'm sure you two will make the most of it.'

'Yeah, well anyway, we'd better go, this hungry

pooch needs food,' Valour said awkwardly, grabbing Sapper by the collar and pulling him away.

'It was great seeing you, Stevie, enjoy your time with your daughter,' he said, walking off.

'No problem, man, take it easy,' Stevie replied, before picking up his saxophone and continuing to play to passers-by.

The pair continued their journey along the boardwalk. Their noses were distracted by the smells and aromas from different cuisines – within a stone's throw there was Chinese, Thai, Japanese, Greek, Jamaican and African food on offer.

'What do you fancy, mate?' Valour asked, looking at Sapper. 'You had Thai yesterday, so maybe try something else.'

Sapper closed his eyes, appearing to meditate. His head moved slowly from side to side, absorbing all the senses. How could he choose just one when they were all smelling so delicious?

The smell of teriyaki chicken was too irresistible. His ears stood up and he barked at the direction of the white Japanese truck with a large red dot on its side.

'Japanese it is then,' Valour said. 'Alright, you know the drill. I can't be a part of this. Go for it. You're on your own.'

Sapper licked his lips and walked towards the

white truck.

About a dozen people gathered around the truck, eating sushi rolls and sipping piping hot miso soup. Sapper looked at them inquisitively, trying to suss out the easiest target.

Two young women who looked like they were in their twenties caught his eye. They giggled as they shared a plate of delicious sushi.

Sapper strolled casually towards them, looking at them with sad eyes, before rolling on his back, hoping to have his belly scratched.

'Wow! Look how cute he is,' the shorter woman said, kneeling down to rub his belly.

'Make room for me too,' her friend agreed, bending down.

'Aww, he must be hungry,' said the shorter woman, as she handed him a huge soft shell crab roll. Sapper grabbed the sushi with his mouth and sprinted off.

He found a quiet spot, out of sight, and wolfed the roll down.

'Feeling better, are we?' Valour asked minutes later, shaking his head. His friend's adventures never ceased to amaze him.

Buuuurrrrpppppp! belched Sapper, looking satisfied with his tongue hanging out.

'I'll take that as yes,' Valour said, smiling. 'You look

like you need a walk to digest those calories!'

Pine trees lined the boardwalk as the pair continued their journey. The sound of waves crashing on the shoreline and the salty smell of the sea caused Sapper to wag his tail vigorously.

He loved the beach—sand between his paws, and salt water on his fur, was paradise.

Valour looked at the beach. It was a familiar sight for him. He'd grown up in Warrior Beach. Loved to body board.

A group of laughing women distracted his thoughts. They were enjoying a game of beach cricket. He loved the game.

'Check out the spin on this,' the bowler said, before running in and bowling the ball. As soon as the tennis ball hit the sand, it spun about a foot to the left. The batsman attempted to hit the ball but missed.

Valour stood still. His jaw dropped in amazement. He closed his eyes. The spinning ball reminded him of a friend from Afghanistan, who he'd met while serving with the army many years prior.

Valour nicknamed her the princess of spin, due to her extraordinary ability to spin the ball and bamboozle batsmen. He would often join in on games in her village, befriending her and her husband.

Valour missed those moments. Every day, he

thought about the couple. Their big smiles, kindness and warmth. He could never forget her eyes — one brown, one green. Valour always told her she was born to be in the army, with camouflage eyes like hers.

The couple had a young son.

Those were distant memories now. A tear ran down his cheek as he reminisced. He would never see them again.

'Look out!' shouted one of the women cricketers. Valour opened his eyes. The tennis ball was hurtling towards his face, going a million miles an hour through the air.

Before he could even blink, a furry figure dived across his face, catching the ball mid-air.

'What a catch!' the bowler yelled. 'Best classic catch I've ever seen.'

Sapper sat there, panting, the tennis ball in his mouth.

'Show off,' Valour said, removing the ball from his mouth and wiping the saliva on his pants before throwing it back.

Sapper had also taken a liking to the game in Afghanistan. Valour's Afghan friends used to say cricket is made for dogs — chasing balls all day, running around in the sun, rolling around on the ground getting dirty.

'Come on, mate. Let's go,' Valour insisted, wiping

away the tears. 'We have an important visit to make.'

They arrived at Warrior Beach Cemetery about twenty minutes later. The sun was wide awake as Valour wiped sweat from his neck.

The cemetery had an eerie feel to it — located at the top of a hill overlooking the ocean. It was overgrown with grass. Some gravestones had fresh flowers resting against them, while others had seen better days.

The pair walked slowly towards a gravestone familiar to them. The walk never got any easier. Each step was more difficult than the previous one.

Each visit felt like it got harder. A sense of dread consumed him as he approached the gravestone.

He took a deep breath and knelt in front of it. He read the wording on it. It said 'IN MEMORY OF PRIVATE JIMMY JACOBS. A LOVING HUSBAND, FATHER AND SOLDIER. REST IN PEACE.'

Today was Jimmy's birthday.

He relived memories of his best mate while staring at the gravestone. They'd known each other since kindergarten. They were inseparable. Played cricket together, joined the army together and served in the Afghanistan War together.

They were basically joined at the hip.

'Miss you, mate,' he said to the gravestone. 'It should have been me that day, not you. I feel so guilty and helpless. I'd give anything to swap places with you. I promised I would look out for your family should anything terrible happen over there, but I've failed you. I'm a bad friend–weak and hopeless.'

A loud humming sound emerged from above. Valour looked up at the sky and saw the camouflage-coloured military helicopter. It looked like an enormous bird, king of the airways.

Its powerful blades ripped through the sky, causing Valour and Sapper's hair to blow uncontrollably.

The sight and sound of the helicopter caused Valour to place his face in his hands and sob uncontrollably. He punched the grass in anger.

It reminded him of Jimmy and the accident when they were deployed overseas. They were always travelling in helicopters in Afghanistan.

His last memory of Jimmy was the sound of the helicopter returning his deceased body from the battlefield back to base in Afghanistan. The sounds of the blades ripping the sky were a permanent reminder of his friend's sacrifice.

Everything changed from that day onwards. Valour wasn't the same man after that. He felt guilty–it should have been him being returned in the helicopter that day, not his friend.

He'd always prided himself on being a good father,

husband and soldier.

His life fell apart after Jimmy died. He left the army shortly after returning to Australia.

He no longer felt like a warrior–more like an imposter whenever he put on his army uniform. He'd lost his purpose in life. That sense of pride and honour when putting on his slouch hat, or marching on Anzac Day, had disappeared.

He struggled to find work after leaving the army. Kept to himself a lot. Barely spoke to his wife and young daughter.

He couldn't even look his daughter in the eye.

Eventually, even sharing the same home and living under the same roof became too difficult. He didn't feel like he belonged there anymore.

Sapper could sense his friend was struggling and climbed onto his lap to comfort him.

Valour gave him a hug, resting his chin on his mate's neck.

He retrieved a letter from his backpack. It was the eulogy he delivered at Jimmy's funeral. He read the contents of it.

To my best mate, Jimmy.

There's something wrong with farewelling such a great human being at such a young age. Jimmy had so much love to give, and offered so much promise.
His life was taken from us too soon.
I'm here today to say thank you.
Thank you. Thank you for being the best friend anyone could ask for. Thank you for your service to our country. Thank you for being an enduring reminder of what's important in life – family and community.
The world is a better place because you were in it. I couldn't have asked for a better friend, soldier and godfather to my daughter.
The strength and bond of your family is testament to the family you built and values you espouse. You leave behind your wife Michelle, daughters Jenny and Victoria and a baby on the way. Your legacy will live on in them.
The world has lost a great man, tremendous father and adoring husband. The army has lost one of its best soldiers, someone who embodied the values of mateship, courage and honesty.
War can be cruel and unfair, but you did not die in vain. You died saving others.
I wouldn't be the man I am today if it weren't for your

friendship. You taught me how to be tougher, more resilient and more compassionate.

Because of you I gained confidence as a teenager. Because of you I joined the army. Because of you I'm a better husband and father.

Having to say goodbye to you today makes this the hardest day in my life but I know you're in a better place now.

I know you'll always be watching over us, keeping us safe.

Saying goodbye today is the hardest thing I've ever had to do and I never expected to have to do it so soon. I thought you'd give me at least another 50 years.

You taught me so much and I'm a better person because of you.

You can be rest assured your legacy and memory will inspire us all to be better people. That is our promise to you.

You'll never be forgotten. You'll always be remembered. Warriors look after each other.

I know heaven is in safe hands with you flying above. Rest in peace, mate.

Valour sat still and closed his eyes for a moment. He opened them and repeatedly re-read one sentence: *You can be rest assured your legacy and memory will inspire us all to be better people. That is our promise to you.*

He was a liar who'd betrayed his friend. He wasn't honouring Jimmy's legacy by being homeless and he certainly hadn't become a better person since delivering that eulogy. Quite the opposite. His life spiralled out of control since leaving the army.

He was a failure who'd let his family and mate down. An embarrassment to the Anzac tradition.

He didn't even stay in touch with Jimmy's family. He wanted to but didn't have the courage.

Valour folded the letter and placed it back in his backpack.

He looked at Sapper. The streets were their home now.

Although life was harder and every day brought new obstacles, he felt at peace. Jimmy wasn't the only army friend he'd lost, but he felt like a part of his soul died that day in Afghanistan as well.

A few others had passed away after returning home from the war. They struggled like Valour. Despite being thousands of kilometres from war, the battle continued for them. It became too much, the demons unbearable.

The demons couldn't be compartmentalised and stored away in a section of one's brain. They were a constant, a stain on the fabric of one's wellbeing.

'Happy birthday, mate, wish you were here,' he whispered to Jimmy's gravestone, kneeling down.

Valour placed his face in his hands and sobbed uncontrollably, as the late afternoon sun shone on his body. The tears flowed like rainwater. He hated the man he'd become but didn't know how to change. Torturing himself each day seemed like fair justice for surviving.

Sapper's attempts to console his companion by rubbing his head against Valour's arms did little to comfort him. 'Excuse me, are you okay?' a woman's voice asked from behind.

'Yeah, yeah, I'm okay. Just having a bad day,' he whimpered, without turning around. His face remained buried in his hands.

'There's nothing wrong with crying. We all do it,' a softer voice said. It sounded like a young girl, which caused Valour to pause. It was a voice of innocence.

He reluctantly stood up and turned around. Sapper stood by his side, wagging his tail.

Valour looked at the two strangers, unsure of why they were being so thoughtful.

The young adolescent-looking girl had short blonde hair and looked up at Valour with sympathetic eyes. She wore a school uniform with black leather shoes in desperate need of a polish.

The older woman standing next to her, who Valour assumed was her mother, had long brunette hair and wore big sunglasses, making her difficult to identify.

Her red shirt was tucked into blue jeans.

The woman stared at Valour, causing him to feel awkward. Her voice sounded familiar. 'Valour, is that you?' she asked.

Valour stared back, wondering if he'd been followed to the cemetery.

'Yes, I'm Valour.'

She removed her sunglasses and walked towards him, so they were now just an arm's length apart.

Tears formed in the woman's eyes. 'I can't believe it's you.'

Valour was speechless. It was Jimmy's widow, Michelle, who he hadn't seen in years.

She and her daughter were also visiting Jimmy's gravestone on his birthday.

'It's good to see you,' Michelle said, wiping away her tears. 'Sorry for crying, I just didn't expect to see you here. It has been so long. I almost didn't recognise you. You've changed so much.'

'It has been long, too long,' Valour said, feeling slightly uncomfortable. He looked like he'd gone to the dogs since they'd last seen each other.

'I thought you moved interstate?'

'We moved back to Warrior Beach last year. I can see you've still got Sapper with you.'

'He looks out for me. I don't know where I'd be without him.'

'Remember me?' the girl interrupted, smiling.

Valour looked down at the girl. 'Sure do, Vicky. You must have grown at least a foot since I last saw you. You'll be taller than your mum soon.'

'Why has your appearance changed so much?'

'Don't be rude,' Michelle said, before Valour could reply. 'We all change our stripes from time to time.'

'We came straight here after picking Vicky up from school. She said she saw Maple today.'

Valour closed his eyes and breathed heavily. He wanted to disappear.

'I'm glad you still visit Jimmy,' Michelle said, sensing his distress. 'You're a true friend. I wish we'd kept in contact after I moved the family following Jimmy's death.'

Valour opened his eyes. 'I don't feel like a friend. I feel like an imposter.'

'I heard you've had a tough time in recent years. It's not fair,' Michelle said.

'No, it is fair,' Valour said, shaking his head.

'What do you mean?'

'I'm getting exactly what I deserve for what happened. I live with the pain every day. Jimmy's grave is an eternal reminder of my failure as a soldier and friend.'

'You can't keep beating yourself up about this. It wasn't your fault.'

'That's easy for you to say. You weren't there that day.'

'No, I wasn't, but I knew Jimmy pretty well and I know he wouldn't want his best mate to be blaming himself for what happened.'

'It should have been me that day, Michelle. This should be my gravestone, not his. Do you know how that makes me feel?'

'I can only imagine, Valour. We all learn to heal.'

'There's no healing for me, just pain and anger.'

Michelle wrapped her right arm around Vicky's shoulder. 'We harbour no ill feelings towards you Valour. You were always good to our family, and we miss having you around. We should catch up more regularly and reflect on the good times we all shared together.'

'I don't know, Michelle. I just can't forgive myself. I'm a changed man. Just look at me.'

'Who cares about the outside, I care about the inside,' Michelle said, placing her right hand over her heart.

'I forgive you.'

Valour stood still. He'd never heard Michelle say that. Hearing those three words filled Valour's head with a mixture of emotions. He was grateful for her kind gesture and felt like a weight had been lifted from his shoulders. Then again, those words weren't going to bring his mate back.

'Thank you, Michelle, that means a lot. I think I should leave and let you guys pay your respects in private. Take care.'

'Come on, Valour. Let's keep talking. We have so much to catch up on,' Michelle pleaded.

'Yeah, Valour, you always promised to share some of your cricketing tips with me. I'm now playing the game,' Vicky said, waving her arms. 'I want to impress my siblings.'

'Not today, guys. Perhaps another time. It was so good to see you both. Sapper and I need to make a move. Enjoy the rest of your day.'

Valour and Sapper left the cemetery, without looking back. They didn't know where they were going next. It didn't matter. They just wanted to escape. Seeing Michelle and Vicky only reminded him of the tragedy he felt responsible for.

'Wait a minute!' a voice yelled out. It was Vicky.

'Go back to your mum,' Valour shouted, walking past gravestones. 'I'm leaving.'

Before he and Sapper could reach the cemetery gates, Vicky ran up beside them and grabbed Valour's left hand. She tugged at it until he stopped.

It worked. He stopped and looked down at Vicky. He couldn't yell at her. She was filled with youthful enthusiasm and boundless optimism. She had Jimmy's eyes and smile.

Valour knelt down and looked her in the eyes.

'What do you want?' he asked.

'I forgive you too,' she replied, giving him a hug.

Before Valour could respond, Vicky sprinted off back to her mum.

Valour lay on the grass and stared at the sky. He couldn't believe what he'd just heard. At that moment, he felt like the only person on earth. Nothing else mattered.

Those words meant so much to him. He'd always blamed himself for robbing Jimmy's children of a future without their dad.

He could only imagine the trauma that would bring on a family.

To hear Vicky say that filled him with an overwhelming sense of happiness and hope.

Perhaps he could be happy again.

CHAPTER 6

Maple looked at the time on her mobile phone. It read 3.30pm. She'd sprinted from school to the beach as soon as the bell rang.

She wiggled her feet in the warm golden sand. She wondered how many grains of sand were beneath her. Must be billions or even trillions.

Sometimes she wished she was a grain of sand – same as the rest, indifferent. Nowadays she felt like a fly in a glass of milk.

As the waves crashed onto the beach, the bright sunshine made the surface of the ocean look like it was littered with sparkling diamonds.

Warrior Beach was her favourite hangout. A place to unwind, be free from life's dramas. She went there whenever she could. The vast, never-ending ocean was an ideal place to feel lost. Home was the last place she wanted to be right now.

She ran her left hand through her black hair and tucked her purple body board under her right arm. Her army camouflage board shorts and a black rash vest were a source of pride and frustration—a life that brought with it a rollercoaster of emotions.

She was about to charge into the surf when a solitary figure emerged from the left.

The teenage looking boy walked towards her, a body board tucked under his arms.

He had wavy black hair and brown skin. His face covered in sandpaper-like stubble.

Her heart raced as the boy approached closer. She recognised him.

It was Mo from school. He'd also received the memo about taking advantage of the summer beach weather.

She thought he looked pretty handsome — tall and lean, his arms more muscular than she recalled.

Mo's eyes swelled with shock and surprise, like he'd won a prize, when he recognised the girl standing a few feet away.

The girl he had the hots for was in the front of him.

He cleared his throat before speaking. 'Hey, you,' he said in an unusually deep voice.

Maple looked at him strangely.

Mo felt so stupid. He was standing next to a girl he'd been wanting to speak to for so long, and all he could do was make a fool out of himself. He had learnt nothing from his experience a few hours prior.

'Hey you,' she replied, smiling. 'What brings you to this part of the world?'

Mo thought his heart was going to burst out of his chest, he was that nervous.

'I've been trying out body boarding. A couple of friends suggested it. Sounds like a bit of fun. Plus, I'm sick of school at the moment. Just had to get out of there as soon as the bell rang.'

'I know how you feel. That mentoring session was such a waste of time.'

'Agreed. Not sure why we got singled out like we're somehow special.'

Maple's eyes scanned Mo up and down. He was a few inches taller.

'Having you there is a no-brainer. You're good at everything. Good student, super cricketer.'

Mo laughed. 'You forgot to mention Afghan refugee. Everyone always loves to hear the refugee perspective,' he said sarcastically.

Maple smiled. 'I heard about your century last weekend. Impressive.'

Although she detested the game, she liked this guy and thought pumping up his tyres might win her some points.

Mo got goose bumps knowing that Maple knew of his achievements.

He laughed, feeling more confident. 'The other side was pretty average, that's all,' he said, shrugging his shoulders. 'As if you can talk. You're the future Matilda soccer star.'

Maple rolled her eyes. She hated talking about soccer and reliving what was now a past life.

'Maybe once upon a time, but not anymore,' she said, shaking her head.

'Why is that? Why would you stop? Don't you want the fame and big bucks?'

'I guess I just got a bit sick of it that's all. There's more to life than kicking a ball.'

'Fair enough. So, I suppose we should try to get some waves before it gets too late.'

Mo scratched his face.

'Why do you grow that stubble on your face anyway?' asked Maple.

Mo felt confused by the question. All his research confirmed girls loved the facial hair. Made men look more masculine.

'Give it another week and you'll be swallowing your words,' he replied, stroking the thin layers of hair.

'Are you sure you're not related to my mum? She's of the same view as you are.'

'Maybe you should listen to her more.'

'Well then, perhaps we should do some body boarding while we're at the beach. Can't catch waves while watching them from the sand.'

'Are you sure you can do this? Can you even swim?' Maple quizzed Mo.

Mo rolled his eyes and shook his head. 'Of course I can silly, I've been in this country a while now. I'm not a complete novice. Don't know what you're talking about.'

Maple looked down at his feet and giggled. 'You do realise we're body boarding, not surfing right?'

Mo had tied the board's strap to his foot instead of his wrist.

His face turned pink from embarrassment. He immediately switched it around. He also made a note in his head to never listen to Dale again, who was probably laughing in his bedroom right now.

Mo wore red board shorts, a blue rash vest and carried an orange body board.

He looked ahead towards the water. The mammoth ocean was a world away from his previous life. It looked like it could suck him up in one swoop. He'd never seen the ocean before arriving in Australia with his mum.

He picked up a seashell from the sand and imitated a cricketer, bowling the shell into the water, before shouting 'Howzat!'

'I can't believe you like that game,' Maple said, shaking her head in dissatisfaction. 'It's so boring, like watching paint dry.'

'That's rubbish,' objected Mo. 'It's the greatest game on earth. One day I'm going to play for Australia. I'll get you tickets so you can watch me.'

Maple smirked. 'I'll make sure I have plans that day. Anyway, wouldn't you rather play for Afghanistan?'

Mo shook his head. 'No way, this is my home now. Has been for some time.'

They both walked towards the water but stopped abruptly when the small waves reached their ankles.

The cold water caused their teeth to chatter.

'Alright, on the count of three, let's rip the band aid off and run and dive in,' Maple said.

'Ah okay,' replied Mo hesitantly, questioning in his head whether he should have chosen another activity today. Truth be told he was scared of sharks. Before he arrived in Australia, a family friend told him to watch out–apparently, teenage kids were their favourite snack. He looked out at the enormous blue ocean.

How many sharks could be out there waiting? he thought to himself.

Maple took a deep breath and shouted, 'One, two, three!' They both ran a few metres and dived head-first under a wave.

They emerged moments later, shivering from the freezing cold water and lay on their bellies on top of their body boards.

Mo spat out sea water. 'Are you sure we're not in Antarctica?' he asked sarcastically, kicking his legs furiously in an attempt to warm his body.

Maple put on a brave face. Although she was also cold, she wanted to look tough in front of her friend. 'Typical Sydney ocean water. By the time it's warm, summer is over. You'll get used to it over time.'

'Remind me why we both chose to body board today?' Mo asked, shivering. His messy black hair resembled that of a wet mop.

'My reason is our Term 4 school report cards are out,' Maple said. 'I'm not a star student like you. I don't want to be anywhere near my mum. She's already read it and is unhappy. I'm just going to cop a spray from her when I get home. I should have stuck a hose in the letterbox to soak and destroyed it.'

'Come on, it can't be that bad,' Mo said. 'You're smart.'

Maple blushed at the compliment. She envied Mo's academic prowess. He was the top Year 10 student at school.

Although they were the same age, they came from different worlds.

'I reckon Mr Dryparsons took joy when he typed up my report card,' Maple said, raising her voice. 'He's probably never typed so many Ds in his life.'

'Who cares what Mr Dry poo and parsley thinks,' Mo replied, smiling.

The pair burst out laughing. That was a common nickname for him. Students often joked about their infamous teacher and his odd personal traits.

His eyebrows were so bushy they looked like a spider's web; and his breath was unbearable and smelt like a sewer.

'Easy for you to say, teacher's pet,' Maple said, splashing Mo in the face with water.

'I'm no teacher's pet!' Mo barked, splashing back even harder. 'I just work hard.'

'Why? What's the point?' Maple asked.

Mo paused for a moment. 'I'm grateful for what I have here. Back in Afghanistan I probably wouldn't have gone to school. We were really poor. Moving here was a chance to start a new life, live a better one. I can walk to school in minutes here, whereas over there I would need to walk kilometres and it wasn't safe.'

'Do you even know where Afghanistan is?' he asked, sceptical of his friend's geography knowledge.

Maple scratched her chin, feeling a bit embarrassed. 'Of course I do,' she replied, awkwardly. She had no idea.

'Where is it?' Mo smirked at her, certain she didn't

know the answer, like most people he met.

Maple shuffled on her board. 'It's, um, far away near New Zealand, right?'

Mo laughed uncontrollably, his hands smacking the water. 'No silly, it's in central Asia, near Pakistan. I'll give you another chance. Do you know our national colours?'

Maple shrugged her shoulders. She didn't bother responding. She didn't care.

'Blue and red,' he said, laughing. My board shorts and rash vest are a bit of a giveaway.'

Maple rolled her eyes. 'Okay, smart boy. What is this? A geography lesson? Let's catch some waves. That's what we're here for.'

A large wave began to emerge in the distance. It grew larger and larger with every second. What initially looked like a small two-foot wave, quickly morphed into a six- foot monster.

Maple showed complete confidence.

As the wave approached, she paddled forward. Maple gripped the board hard and let the wave guide her down. The wind blew through her hair. Her eyes were wide open as she rode the wave at incredible speed.

'Wooooo!' she yelled as the wave turned into white water and she approached the shoreline. She lay on her back in the shallow water, taking in the moment.

She was so happy. 'I am the captain of my soul,' she whispered to herself, as water rushed over her body.

Those were the last words written in a letter from her dad. She'd found it on her pillow the day he left. Maple stared at the sky, repeating those words in her head.

Now it was Mo's turn. He was in awe of what he'd just witnessed. Maple looked like a pro, effortlessly catching the gigantic wave.

He took a large gulp. He was scared. Coming from a landlocked country, this was a new activity for him. He was far away from the dusty, desolate villages of Afghanistan.

A wave approached. He felt a sense of relief when he saw how small it was.

The relief was short-lived. The wave transformed rapidly. One second it was the height of a small ladder, the next second it was the height of a house — a large house.

His heart raced as his body reached the top of the wave. He felt like he was looking down from the top of a building.

'Whoooaa!' he screamed as the board descended. He felt like he was falling off a building. Unlike Maple, he didn't grip the board and lost control almost immediately.

He tumbled down the wave, the water swallowing him. His body twisted and turned like he was inside a washing machine as the waves crashed around him.

He emerged from the water, flapping his arms like a fish out of water. He rubbed his eyes and coughed out water.

'Nice work, buddy,' Maple said, clapping her hands, laughing.

'Zip it!' Mo exclaimed. 'It's easy for you. You grew up with this as your backyard.'

'Come on Mo, don't give up just yet,' Maple said. 'You can't let the wave control you, you must control it.'

Mo looked confused. What on earth was she saying?

The pair paddled back out and spent the next twenty minutes catching more waves, with Mo putting on a brave face. He was out of his comfort zone. He couldn't control the waves the same way he could control a cricket bat and ball.

'I'm feeling pretty thirsty after all that exercise,' Mo said, puffing after almost nailing a big wave.

'Just have some sea water,' replied Maple, smirking. 'It tastes just like lemonade.'

'Are you sure?' asked Mo, looking bewildered.

'Sure is, it's delicious,' Maple said.

Mo took a large gulp of sea water, using his right

hand as a cup, immediately spitting the salty water out.

'Ahhh! That's disgusting!' he yelled, using his fingers to scrape the salty taste out of his mouth.

'Are you sure you're the Dux at school?' Maple asked sarcastically.

Mo looked at Maple angrily, with snake-like eyes. He grabbed a pile of seaweed that was floating next to him and threw it at her, causing her to fall off her body board.

Maple emerged from the water with the seaweed hanging over her head.

'Ha! You look like an octopus,' he said, laughing.

'Alright, we're even,' replied Maple, removing the seaweed from her head.

A loud humming sound approached overhead. They looked up and saw a camouflage-coloured military helicopter.

The sight reminded Maple of her dad and his military service. She missed him.

Mo looked down at Maple's legs. 'Your board shorts match that helicopter,' he said, pointing at her shorts.

'Yeah, they were a gift from my dad. He used to be in the army.'

Mo's mouth opened wide in excitement. 'Wow! That's awesome,' he said cheerfully. 'Being a soldier would be pretty cool. What did he do in the army?'

Maple scratched the back of her head, feeling uneasy. 'He was a combat engineer. He used to clear explosives.'

'Sounds cool. Dangerous I suppose. I have a lot of respect for those guys. Putting themselves on the line for their country. Risking everything in defence of our values.'

'What are you guys doing for the school holidays?'

Maple looked expressionless. Her stomach dropped. She'd been dreading this topic. Over the past week, there were constant reminders of it–TV ads, shops offering discounts on goods.

It was hard for her, not having her dad around. She felt different, like an outsider. She recalled the day when he gave her the camouflage board shorts. She was so happy. Now she too could look like a soldier. She used to brag to friends about her dad's military service. Not anymore. They hadn't seen each other in a few years.

She didn't know where he was now or if he was even alive.

She had to help her mum around the house a lot more now with her dad gone–taking out the rubbish, assisting with cooking and cleaning. It wasn't easy. She often cried alone in her bedroom at night, longing for her dad to return home.

'Not much, just hanging out with parents this afternoon,' she replied, eventually, biting her bottom lip and finding it difficult to lie.

'Yeah, me too,' Mo said. 'It's a hard time for Mum and me. Not the same without Dad.'

'What do you mean?' asked Maple, looking surprised.

'My dad died a while ago. While we were living in Afghanistan. Mum raised me on her own since then. It's just the two of us now. I have memories of him but it's hard without him. Mum doesn't like to talk about it. I wish I knew more about him.'

Maple had no idea. Then again, she'd never bothered to introduce herself to Mo.

During that moment, she didn't feel alone. Who would have thought, the guy from another universe is the one person who could relate to her?

'You know my mum told me people in my village back home used to always rave about the Australian soldiers, especially those like your dad who cleared explosives from the ground,' Mo said proudly.

'Why?' Maple asked.

Mo shook his head vigorously from side to side, to clear his mind, water flying everywhere. 'They saved lives. Made the villages safer. They're heroes.'

Maple felt confused. If they're heroes, then why

did her dad leave? she wondered. What sort of hero abandons his family when they need him the most? Aren't heroes supposed to embrace challenges, not walk away from them?

'So, what's your background by the way, I've never asked?' Mo asked.

'Half Aussie, half Chinese,' Maple replied, stroking her black hair. 'My mum is Chinese Australian.'

'Nice,' Mo replied. 'That's another thing I love about this place – its diversity. All you have to do is go for a short walk and you stumble across people from all backgrounds.'

The word diversity wasn't just a catchphrase for Mo, it was a way of life, a badge of pride. Back in Afghanistan, being different could get you or your family killed, whereas in Australia it was a cultural asset.

'So why did you quit soccer?' asked Mo. 'You were so good at it.'

'I don't know, man. I was a bit over all the pressure and stress of it. Seemed a bit pointless to me. It's not like I would have gone very far with it.'

'That's not what I've heard,' Mo said, shaking his head. 'I'm told you have a gift. You shouldn't waste it.'

'What do you know?' she asked, raising her voice in objection. 'You don't know me.'

'Hey don't blame me. I'm just telling you the facts. You keep to yourself at school most of the time. People say you've changed over the last couple of years.'

Maple slapped the water in anger. 'People, you say. Who? That idiot friend of yours, Dale? What would he know? People should mind their own business.'

Mo raised his hands in a surrender like pose. 'Okay, okay. Calm down. I agree, people should mind their own business. And yes, Dale is an idiot.'

Maple laughed and smiled at Mo.

She felt comfortable around him. Like she could unwind and be sincere.

A ripple in the water distracted the pair. The ripple became larger, bubbles coming to the surface.

'Did you just fart?' Maple asked, disapprovingly.

Mo was shocked. 'No way!' he retorted. 'I bet it was you. You've been holding it in this whole time.'

A small nose appeared from the water, followed by a pair of eyes and ears. A furry four-legged black coloured amphibious creature began doggie paddling towards Maple and Mo.

'That dog is a good swimmer,' Mo said, as it paddled up to him.

'What's its name?' Maple asked, pointing at its collar.

Mo leaned over and looked at the collar. 'It says his name is Sapper,' Mo said. The dog paddled over to Maple.

Maple felt butterflies in her stomach. 'Did you say Sapper?' she asked, excitedly.

'That's what I said,' Mo replied, looking confused. 'What's the big deal?'

'Sapper used to live with us, then one day he disappeared,' she said, unable to contain her excitement, scratching the dog's nose. 'I haven't seen him in a few years.'

'What sort of name is Sapper anyway?' asked Mo.

'It's a nickname given to military combat engineers,' replied Maple. 'Like my dad'.

Mo joined in on the excitement and began patting Sapper.

'He's no ordinary dog,' Maple said. 'Not your typical pet.'

'How so?' asked Mo.

'He also served in the army,' Maple said.

'Yeah right, as if,' Mo said. 'Why would the army want a furry ball of fluff like Sapper?'

'Well, you know how you were saying the army combat engineers kept villages safe from explosions?' asked Maple.

'Yes,' replied Mo, unsure where the conversation was going.

Maple continued. 'Dogs like Sapper were the

soldiers' biggest weapon. They were used to sniff out explosives in the ground so they could then be safely removed. Sapper was my dad's dog over there. They worked together to keep villages safe.'

Mo's jaw dropped in shock. 'Wow,' he said. He was lost for words. 'So what happened when they left the war?'

'My dad and Sapper were so close that the army let us keep him after Dad left the army,' Maple said.

'Come to think of it, my mum did tell me a story once of an army dog she came across in Afghanistan.'

It then dawned on Maple. If Sapper was here, then maybe her dad was nearby. He took Sapper with him when he left a few years ago.

Maple felt uneasy. She asked herself questions in her mind — what would she say if she saw him? How would he react? Tears filled her eyes. She was overcome with emotion.

'What's the matter?' Mo asked, feeling sorry for his new friend.

'It's nothing, just got some of that seaweed in my eye. It's no big deal,' she replied, rubbing her eyes.

Sapper turned towards the shoreline and swam off.

'Hey, come back, Sapper, where are you going?' Maple yelled. She didn't want to lose him again.

His little legs kicked furiously in the water. Maple

didn't stand a chance of catching him as he caught onto a wave.

She watched as he reached the shoreline and shook his body, causing water to fly in every direction. He then sprinted off onto the boardwalk, out of sight.

Maple looked down at her reflection in the water. She wore a sombre expression on her face.

The day her dad and Sapper left, she ran to the bathroom and stared in the mirror, looking for answers.

'Was there something wrong with me?' she asked herself at the time. 'What did I do to cause this?'

Tears flowed down her cheeks as she recalled that day.

That must be some bad seaweed, if it makes you cry, Mo thought to himself. He looked around, making sure there was none near him.

'I don't know about you, but I'm starving,' Mo said, trying to cheer her up. 'Do you like hot dogs? My mum works at the local hot dog restaurant. We can go there for dinner. I know it's nursing home hours, but I'm getting hungry.'

Maple looked at Mo with reddened eyes. 'Yeah, I love hot dogs. Let's eat,' she replied, attempting to smile.

'Awesome. Let's get out of here while the waves are still small. I don't want to feel like I'm in a blender again,' Mo said, making a bolt for the shoreline. Maple followed.

They shook sand off their towels and brushed their wet bodies.

Mo picked up his mobile phone. He'd received a text. It read:

Hey Mo, thanks for today. I'm looking forward to our next mentoring session. My mum says she's always seeing your name come up in the school bulletin for sports and academics, so I bet I can learn a lot from you – Vicky.

Vicky's response took Mo by surprise. He thought he'd scared her off, not inspired her.

A sense of gratitude and appreciation swept through his body.

He replied to the text.

Hi Vicky,

Good to hear from you. I enjoyed meeting you as well.

This mentoring program is different from anything I've ever experienced.

To be honest, I was a bit sceptical about it, but after our first session, I can see why it was established.

I'm sure we'll learn more about each other as the program progresses.

Looking like a quiet holiday for me. Not going anywhere. I'll probably hit the cricket nets a bit.

I'm currently at the beach. Been learning how to body

board. I think I'll stick to cricket lol.

Anyway I guess I'll see you next week for our next session.

Cheers

Mo

Mo put his phone away and collected his things. 'I'm going to go change. Let's meet on the boardwalk and we can walk from there?' he suggested.

'Sure, I won't be long.'

Maple pulled her phone from her bag and checked her emails. She expected an unpleasant email from her mum.

She never understood why her mum didn't text, always emailed her.

As expected, there was a new email from her mum. She took a deep breath before opening it.

Maple darling,

Where are you? You're supposed to be home by now doing your chores.

We need to talk. Your behaviour is becoming unacceptable.

You report card is the worst I've seen from you.

You can do better than this. You have so much potential darling. Don't waste it.

Call me when you can. I just want to know you're safe.
Love Mum xox

Maple gritted her teeth in anger. A wave of emotions passed through her mind. Mostly frustration and fury, but also a sense of understanding. She did have enormous potential and she knew it.

She clicked reply to the email and wrote back.

Mum,

Take it easy. I'm at the beach like I said.

I won't be home for dinner. Don't worry, I'm safe. I'm with friends.

No one cares about report cards anymore. Sorry I'm not perfect like you.

I'll see you later.

Maple

Maple threw the phone in her bag and stormed off to the change room.

CHAPTER 7

Mariam mopped the floor of the women's bathroom. Her arms ached from the labour. She was a perfectionist and took her job as a cleaner at Warrior Dogs Restaurant seriously.

She refused to leave any smudge or mark on the floor. She wanted it to be so shiny she could see her reflection in it. Her motto was if you're going to do something, do it properly.

It wasn't a simple task. Earlier that day a group of girls challenged their friend to eat five hot dogs in a minute.

The girl took on the challenge, munching the hot dogs like it was her last meal. She looked like a hungry dingo feeding on its prey.

The girl achieved the feat, much to her friends' surprise.

An amazing accomplishment, or at least the girl thought. One minute she was being hailed as some kind of hero by her friends, the next minute she was sprinting to the bathroom to eject her achievement in the toilet, while a friend held her hair back.

Mariam was left to clean up the mess.

She used her left elbow to wipe a bead of sweat from her forehead. It was tough work. She never complained.

She looked down at the mop. A simple, long, unimpressive looking stick.

Not for Mariam. It was more than that. It symbolised a new chapter in life – new opportunities, new challenges.

Mariam finished the task, dropped the mop and looked at herself in the mirror. She was alone.

Alone because of the sign she had placed outside the bathroom which read 'DO NOT ENTER. CLEANING IN PROGRESS'.

She'd never possessed such power before. Never been in a position where she could dictate what other people can and cannot do.

Growing up in Afghanistan, she had been afforded few opportunities. Raised in a dusty, impoverished village, she never went to school and had no job prospects.

Her light blue cleaning uniform was something very different from what she would wear in her former homeland. She was now part of something, an equal.

A navy blue headscarf covered her long black hair.

She stared at the bathroom mirror. She was a world away from her old life, which could have turned out very differently. Mariam closed her eyes and thought back to a day in Afghanistan many years prior. A day that would be etched in her mind forever. A day filled with mixed emotions.

The heat was unforgiving. A form of torture. An enemy in its own right that didn't discriminate against race, gender or creed. It was one of the few guarantees in this isolated part of the world. A beast that couldn't be tamed.

The sun wouldn't be setting for a few hours.

Only the toughest, most resilient humans could withstand this challenge. Every summer in Afghanistan was a test of stamina and endurance. You never got used to it.

Mariam stared at the blue stained sky, wondering when the enemy would lay down its arms for the day and provide a few hours of respite.

Unlike the enemy that had haunted her countrymen for years, this enemy was seasonal, not omnipresent.

Her village wasn't immune from violence and distress. The week prior, an improvised explosive device exploded, killing two children and injuring several others.

The incident was still raw in her mind. She knew the families of the deceased and injured. Images of bloodshed just couldn't be erased. The screams that came from their loved ones were a stain on her mind — a powerful reminder of the horrors of war and the surrender of innocence.

Lives cut short far too soon. It didn't seem fair. Then again, nothing seemed fair in this country.

Extreme poverty, the lack of human rights, few economic opportunities, terrorism — these weren't just labels — they defined people's lives. There was no escaping it.

There was also no time for dwelling on it either. That was life in this part of the world that had received one too many doses of hardship and brutality.

Each day brought new challenges. You couldn't rely on clean drinking water and electricity in this part of the world.

Worn out looking village shops with tin roofs straddled the main dusty road a few hundred metres away. Men and women sat behind wooden tables selling an assortment of goods, including food and clothing.

The complete opposite of Australia's Western economy, with its lavish shopping centres, abundance of cafes and nightlife.

It was a humble life, but the locals never complained. They were grateful for what they had.

Mariam looked straight ahead at the makeshift dirt

cricket pitch.

It was a far cry from the Sydney Cricket Ground.

'Come on Mariam, we don't have all day,' a voice called out.

She looked at her right hand, holding a tennis ball. Mariam gripped it hard.

She lifted her head and looked at a male soldier dressed in desert camouflage uniform and wearing sunglasses, standing about twenty feet away, holding a cricket bat and standing in front of a rubbish bin, which doubled as a set of stumps.

The hard dirt ground served as the pitch. Children from around the village helped as fielders. The heat didn't seem to bother them. They loved cricket. Their colourful clothes emulated a sense of hope and optimism.

'Show us this googly you've been boasting about,' the man insisted.

Mariam took a few deep breaths and rubbed the ball against the palm on her left hand.

She wasn't exactly dressed for the occasion, wearing a loose-fitting black shirt, olive green pants and a black headscarf.

Mariam didn't care. She just wanted to play the game.

She walked slowly up to a line in the ground, which

was a makeshift crease, rolled her arm over her head, and flicked her wrist, before releasing the ball.

The spinning ball flew towards the soldier. His tongue hung from his mouth as the ball dropped on the ground, picking up dust along the way. The soldier placed his left foot forward and played a straight bat, hoping to hit the ball back past the bowler.

The children took a collective deep breath.

To the batsman's dismay, the ball bamboozled him, with its incredible spin causing him to miss it altogether and hitting the rubbish bin stumps instead.

Mariam threw her arms in the air and screamed with excitement. Any discomfort from the raging heat was forgotten in that split second. She was overcome with happiness.

The children cheered. Some jumped up and down, while others sprinted towards Mariam, pulling at her arms, looking at her with adulation. They treated her like a hero.

'Got him!' another male soldier yelled from midwicket. 'Jimmy, you had no idea what was going on there. Gotta watch the ball, mate. You've always struggled with spin.'

Jimmy remained in his batting stance, shaking his head in amazement.

'Unbelievable,' he said, pointing the bat at his

friend. 'You think this is easy, Valour. Come and try yourself.'

'No, mate, you can be the only one who makes a fool out of himself today,' Valour replied. 'I know better than to face one of Mariam's spinners.'

Jimmy wiped sweat from his neck and walked towards Mariam, who seemed to be enjoying the limelight.

That tennis ball was more than just a round figure covered in yellow fluff. It was a source of freedom and aspiration. Growing up under the Taliban she wasn't afforded such freedoms and could only dream of playing the game.

'Where's our four-legged fielder?' Jimmy asked.

Valour looked towards a large tree providing copious shade and saw his black Labrador napping under a branch.

He was enjoying a well-earned rest.

'Come here, Sapper, rest time is over, mate.'

Sapper raised his head reluctantly, looking half asleep.

'Cut it out, mate, he deserves a break, after everything he's done,' Jimmy said. 'Let him nap.'

Jimmy was right. Sapper wasn't a pet. He was a war dog.

Selected to join the army two years ago, he blitzed

his training and quickly established himself as one of the military's most sought-after bomb detection dogs.

He was a platoon's life saver–sniffing out explosives before they detonated, so Valour and his team could deactivate them safely.

He was a soldier's best mate and villagers welcomed him with open arms. He gave them hope and confidence. A voiceless hero.

Valour shook his head. 'No way, he's been napping for more than an hour now. We need to get back to base.'

'Come on boy, time to get going. You can keep snoozing there.'

Sapper yawned, struggled to his feet and walked slowly towards his commander. The look in his eyes was one of disapproval. He would have enjoyed a longer nap.

Valour retrieved a water bottle from his backpack, allowing Sapper to enjoy some precious drops of liquid gold.

All three circled around him, admiring the sight. They wondered how someone so special could make such awful slurping sounds when drinking. Sapper consumed that water like it was his last drink.

His coat was covered in dust–his own form of camouflage.

'That's one thirsty boy,' a deep voice said.

The trio turned around and were greeted by Abdul, Mariam's husband. He wore traditional Afghan clothing, consisting of a long black tunic shirt that reached his knees, loose white trousers, black sandals and a white turban. His face was covered in a thick, black beard.

Standing alongside him was their young son, Mohammed, wearing a loose-fitting blue tunic top, with blue trousers and black sandals. A round red cap adorned his thick black hair.

Valour and Jimmy beamed at the father and son. It never ceased to amaze them that, despite how advanced and modernised other countries were, Afghanistan somehow managed to preserve its customs and traditions, including fashion.

'I don't how you guys can wear that clothing in this heat,' Valour said, surveying their bodies head to toe.

'If I were you, I'd be wearing shorts and a t-shirt.'

Abdul shook his head while smiling. 'Then again, my friend, you'd be nursing your burnt skin in the evening.'

'How's our furry warrior going then?' Abdul asked.

'Are you referring to the dog or that rug on your face, dear?' Mariam asked.

Abdul laughed, shaking his head at Valour and

Sapper. 'I don't know why she complains so much, fellas, most men have beards over here.'

'I'm with you on this one,' Valour said. 'My wife hates them too. Won't let me grow one. Says it gives her a face rash when I kiss her.'

'Maybe I need to get your wife to call Abdul then and give him some advice. Kissing him is like having a piece of sandpaper wiped over me,' Mariam said.

Valour stroked Sapper's back, trying to wipe the dust off. 'I'll be sure to do that Mariam.'

'Now to your question, Abdul, Sapper's been snoozing while your lovely wife has been taking wickets all afternoon.'

Abdul laughed. 'I keep telling her you guys have real work to do and she should stop bothering you.'

'Never mind, mate, I never miss an opportunity to roll the arm over.'

'Sorry to hear about last week,' Valour said, changing the subject.

The expression on Abdul's face went from a smile to a frown. 'Thank you, my friend. It was a massive blow to this community. So many families devastated. The future of this country rests with our younger generations and now there's a few less to guide us going forward. But we'll somehow get through it. This country is used to overcoming adversity.'

Tears filled Mariam's eyes. She knelt down and hugged her son, who was too young to understand the nature of the conversation.

'Certainly is,' Jimmy said. 'But that's why we're here. To help. Standing up and getting on with life, despite how hard that may seem when confronted by unimaginable tragedy, is a powerful weapon against the Taliban's sinister forces.'

Valour nodded. 'He's right. We may not be here every day, but this village is a top priority for us, including keeping you all safe. Read my lips–we won't turn our backs on you.'

Abdul placed his left hand on Valour's right shoulder, looking him in the eyes. 'You are both good men. You have no idea how grateful we all are for your work. If it wasn't for people like you, Mariam and these kids wouldn't even be able to play cricket. You're making a difference. People do tell me though that the Taliban is ramping up its activities in this region.'

Abdul pulled a letter out of his right pocket and handed it to Valour. 'I want you to have this, my friend. Don't read it now. Read it when you feel overcome with pain and despair.'

Valour thanked Abdul, then placed the letter in his backpack, slightly taken aback by his friend's approach.

'Rest assured, mate, I'll be back here with Sapper tomorrow,' he said. 'You can count on it. We'll redouble our efforts if we have to.'

Abdul smiled. 'You're too kind, my friend.'

'What about you, Jimmy?'

Jimmy stretched his arms out and yawned. 'I won't be here tomorrow, mate. I'm having a break. Sapper is more useful anyway.'

'That's because he has two more legs than you,' Abdul said.

A soft buzzing sound emerged from across the horizon, with the sound becoming louder and more aggressive each second.

The group looked towards the sound and saw the military helicopter approach the field.

Valour and Jimmy looked at each other. It was time to leave. Their transport had arrived.

The chopper landed near the makeshift cricket pitch, causing a dust storm. It looked like a giant bird, its modern technological warfare capabilities a stark contrast to the humble Afghan village.

Few villagers took much notice. The Australian Army was practically a part of the community.

Mohammed hid behind his mum, clinging to her legs, afraid of the mighty roar and physical presence of the chopper.

The soldier guarding Valour and Jimmy's rifles ran over to them. 'It's time to go, guys,' he said, before running towards the chopper.

'Enjoy the rest of your day,' Valour said to Abdul, Mariam and Mohammed.

'Maybe you can face one of my spinners tomorrow,' Mariam said, rolling her right arm over.

'Looking forward to it. Remember what I said— we've got your backs. We won't let you down.'

Abdul wrapped his arms around his wife and son, watching on as Valour, Jimmy and Sapper jumped onto the chopper and flew off into the horizon.

Mariam opened her eyes and stared at the bathroom mirror. She wiped away tears from her face. Thinking back to that day was never easy.

She ran the fingers on her right hand over the wristband on her left hand. She smiled.

The wristband was that of her local cricket club— the Warrior Beach Wombats. Cricket was her favourite sport. She loved it.

She stared at the mirror. One eye was green, while the other was brown. They had reddened. She hadn't slept much that night. She had tossed and turned in bed, anxious about the upcoming festive season and school holidays. It brought back so many memories— joyful and sad.

She missed her husband and longed to see him again. Just one last time. She wished she could talk to her son about him more, share some of her happiest memories, but every time she tried, she became overwhelmed with emotion.

There was a bulge in both her left and right pockets. She placed her hand in her left pocket and removed a folded bit of paper. It was her son's Year 10 report card from Warrior Beach High School.

She unfolded the paper and gazed at it. Straight As. She'd never seen so many As in her life.

She was so proud of him and wondered what sort of life he would have lived if they'd remained in Afghanistan.

The aches and pains that came with her work were all worth it. Any regrets she may have had about moving to this sun burnt country disappeared at the sight of that simple bit of paper.

She then removed a rolled-up piece of paper from her right pocket. It was a letter she received years ago from her Australian soldier friend Valour in Afghanistan. She read the last words in the letter: 'You are the captain of your soul,' it said. Those few words had always provided her with hope and inspiration, despite facing all kinds of challenges in life.

Her thoughts were interrupted by the bathroom

door opening. 'Hey Mariam, can you throw the rubbish out, please?' her manager asked.

'Sure thing, boss,' she replied.

She left the bathroom and walked through the kitchen to collect the rubbish.

The restaurant was packed that day. One of the most popular places in the neighbourhood, famed for its delicious hot dogs.

All meals were half price for the holidays. Children were there with their parents, pulling their arms, begging for their favourite food.

A lot of parents were holding cards their children had made for them at school, inscribed with all kinds of thoughtful words. Their faces wore big smiles.

Mariam picked up two big rubbish bags, walked out into the alleyway and dumped them into the bin.

She stretched her arms out, causing her joints to crack.

She took a few steps forward and lifted her left arm over her head. She then rolled her right arm over her shoulder and head, rotating her wrist at the end. She was practising her cricket bowling.

'Got him!' shouted a man walking by, giving her the thumbs up.

Mariam blushed, her face turning pink.

As she turned to enter the restaurant, the humming

sound of an aircraft distracted her.

She looked up at the darkening blue sky, as the sun slowly set. A camouflage-coloured military helicopter tore through it.

Its blades were so loud it sounded like a thousand blenders going off at once.

Its green, black and brown colours were confronting but somehow comforting. What was it doing? Mariam thought to herself. Who was in it and why?

It was a familiar sight for her back in Afghanistan. Military helicopters were as common as cars.

They were a source of security and help.

The sight and sound brought back a memory. A day that was forever etched in her mind. A day that changed her life.

'I am the captain of my soul,' she whispered to herself, tears running down her face. She wiped them, collected herself and went back into the restaurant.

She mopped the floor near a row of booths, still distracted by the earlier sound. She looked down at the floor, fixated on the task at hand.

'Hi Mum,' a young deep voice called out from the restaurant entrance.

Mariam looked up. It was her son, Mo. He had a female friend with him, dressed in a tank top, denim skirt and sandals.

His hair was wavy and uncombed. Similar to the mop she was holding. He was wearing shorts, a t-shirt and thongs.

She winked at her son, attempting to show how impressed she was with his choice in women.

He wasn't impressed. Mo shook his head slowly at his mum, not even blinking.

'Hi, guys, come in and sit down. My shift ends in half an hour. I'll get you some dinner,' she said, pointing to an empty booth next to a window.

The pair sat down.

'How was the beach?' Mariam asked, looking at the water dripping from her son's hair.

'Yeah, it was good fun,' he boasted. 'Caught some huge waves with my friend Maple here from school.'

Maple smirked and rolled her eyes. 'He's a pro for sure,' she said, winking at Mariam.

Mariam smiled. Clearly they both knew Mo loved to exaggerate things, especially his athletic prowess.

'I'm Mo's mum, hope you like hot dogs.'

'Love them. One of my favourite foods,' replied Maple, rubbing her hands together. 'I'm starving.'

'You've come to the right place,' Mo said, picking up a menu. 'Best hot dogs in the world right here.'

Their food arrived about ten minutes later. Maple ordered a vegetarian dog, while Mo ordered a cheese and pickle one.

Before they could dig in, Mariam said to Mo while mopping, 'You know your dad liked hot dogs, but chilli ones.'

Mo stared at the food. He had no idea. 'Why don't you add some chilli and give it a go?' asked Maple, handing Mo a bottle of the stuff.

Mo shrugged his shoulders. 'Sure, bit of spice never hurt anyone.'

Mo began to pour the chilli sauce on the hot dog. Both Maple and Mariam's eyebrows rose in surprise when they saw just how much he was pouring. It was like he was laying cement on the thing.

'Hey, not too much, Mo,' Mariam hesitated, with a concerned look on her face. 'You don't want to set your mouth on fire.'

'Chill out, Mum, I know what I'm doing, it's just a bit of chilli,' replied Mo defiantly. He found it embarrassing whenever his mum challenged him in front of others.

He picked up the hot dog. Maple covered her mouth with her hands in anticipation.

Mo took a large bite and chewed. Maple and Mariam breathed a sigh of relief from Mo's lack of reaction.

It didn't last long. Mo suddenly stopped chewing.

His mouth stood still, his face turning purple, covered in sweat.

His eyes began to water, his body trembled. He spat the food out and stood up.

'Uhhhhhh!' he screamed, as the chilli's force took hold of his mouth. It was so hot it felt like a volcano was exploding in his mouth.

'Out of my way, out of my way!' he yelled, running up and down the restaurant, pushing customers out of the way, looking for help.

He spotted the bucket of water his mum was using to mop the floor. At that moment, it looked like a river of water.

He ran to the bucket and knelt down. Before he put his hands in, Maple intervened.

'Take this!' she cried out, grabbing a banana milkshake from an overweight man seated nearby.

'Hey give that back kid!' the overweight man shouted.

Mo held the milkshake with both hands and consumed it. He didn't stop until it was empty.

He huffed and puffed afterwards, using his sleeve to wipe his mouth.

The entire restaurant burst out laughing.

Mo stared at the putrid sight on the floor. It looked like a pile of vomit. He'd not only disgraced himself, but also his family. His mum would be left to clean up the mess.

To make matters worse, he'd made a fool out of himself in front of the girl he fancied.

He didn't think about that before he took on the challenge – he was only thinking of himself.

'Nice work, kid,' the overweight man said, before laughing.

He wasn't the only one sledging Mo. Adults and children both sniggered away in their booths, making fun of him.

Mo felt humiliated as he stumbled back to the table, a frown covering his face. He'd never been so embarrassed in his life. He was so used to being on top–generating applause and cheers from crowds of people.

'At least you know a bit more about your dad,' Maple said, patting him on the back. 'Although I get the impression he wouldn't have reacted like that.'

Mo looked at her with those steely eyes, like a snake. He wasn't in the mood for jokes.

It wasn't his finest hour. He'd never felt so ridiculous.

'Just eat your tofu dog!' he snapped.

'Don't mind if I do,' replied Maple, taking a bite of it and swallowing. 'This dog is so good, best ever,' she teased.

Mariam rushed over to the scene and mopped the floor. Every stroke of the mop was like a dagger through Mo's chest. His mum made so many sacrifices for him and this is how he repaid her.

Mariam could sense her son's frustration and walked over after cleaning up the mess.

'You want to know something else about your dad?' she asked.

'Not if it almost kills me again.'

Mariam sat down opposite the pair. 'Your dad used to be in the army.'

Mo looked up. His eyes widened with interest. 'The army!' he exclaimed. 'So, he was a soldier?'

'That's correct,' Mariam replied. 'He was an interpreter for the Australian Army. He helped keep the community safe and saved lives.'

Mo felt butterflies in his stomach — he was overcome with pride. His frown turned into a smile.

'Wow. So, he's like your dad then, Maple?' he asked, turning to face his friend.

Maple nodded, only half listening. She was still distracted by her delicious hot dog.

Mariam's eyes widened with interest. 'Your dad was in the army?' she asked.

Maple swallowed her food and looked at Mariam. 'Yeah, he was. Served in Afghanistan.'

'That's wonderful. You should bring him in here for a meal sometime. I'd love to meet him.'

'Ah yeah, maybe,' replied Maple awkwardly, wishing the conversation would end soon.

'What does he like doing?' Mariam asked.

'Cricket,' replied Maple.

Mariam's mouth opened wide in disbelief. 'Cricket! I love cricket!'

Oh boy, thought Maple. Here we go.

'I even dream about it,' she said. 'It was an Australian soldier who taught me how to play, in fact. He also taught Mo's dad.'

Maple and Mo looked at her with puzzled eyes.

'When I was growing up, there weren't many sporting opportunities, especially in the rural villages,' Mariam said.

'But during the war, we achieved greater freedom. We used to play games against the soldiers. It was so much fun.'

Mariam chuckled to herself, thinking back to those memories.

She sensed her presence was embarrassing the pair and left the table, resuming her mopping.

Maple looked out the window to the alleyway. The sound of someone rifling through a bin caught her attention.

She looked to the source of the sound and saw a dishevelled-looking man rummaging through the bin filled with waste. He looked in desperate need of a shower.

Leftover hot dogs and soggy fries covered the top of the trash.

The man had long brown hair and a long beard. Why wouldn't he just come in for food? Why would anyone want to eat food from a bin? she wondered.

The man wore an army backpack and camouflage pants, but didn't look anything like a soldier. He looked like a beast.

Maple was about to turn back around and resume eating, when an item protruding from the backpack caught her eye.

It was a teddy bear, its head sticking out from the top.

She stared at the bear. There was something different about it. Something special.

Then she noticed the purple ribbon around its neck. Her favourite colour. Her dad had given her a similar bear before he went to Afghanistan, when she was much younger.

It was her favourite toy. Never went to bed without it. It reminded her of her dad, and provided her with a sense of hope and optimism whenever he was away for army work.

Then one day a few years ago it disappeared, without a trace. Not seen since.

There must be a few of those bears around, she thought, as she stared at it.

As the man leaned forward further into the bin to retrieve food, the bear fell out of his backpack.

Maple's jaw dropped in surprise.

'What is it? What have you seen?' asked Mo.

The bear had a big 'M' printed on its belly. It was her bear.

'That man has my favourite teddy bear!' Maple said, feeling agitated.

'How do you know it's yours?' asked Mo, peering out the window. 'There are a million bears like that.'

'Not with the letter 'M' on it and a purple ribbon around its neck,' she said. 'I was devastated when it disappeared.'

'Check out his beard. You could make a blanket out of that thing,' Mo said.

They both giggled.

'You thinking what I'm thinking?' Mo asked.

'What's that?'

'Let's get your bear back,' Mo said, winking.

'I don't know, man. We don't know this guy. He could be dangerous. What if he attacks us?'

'Come on, there are two of us, plus if things get heated, we can run back to the restaurant. How much does that bear mean to you?'

'It means the world to me. It carries so many memories.'

'How does it make you feel that someone else has something you adore?'

Maple stared at the bear.

'I think you know what we need to do,' Mo said.

Maple nodded furiously.

CHAPTER 8

Maple and Mo tippy-toed outside into the alleyway, trying to avoid making noise.

A cool breeze brushed over their faces.

The area was darkening, making it feel lonelier and intimidating.

They felt like they were on some clandestine operation, communicating in hand signals rather than words.

They crept closer and closer to the bin, assuming the strange man was behind it.

Their hearts raced as they got closer.

'Ehhhhh!'

A loud screeching sound emerged from behind the bin, causing them to jump in the air and fall on their back sides.

A feral cat bolted off.

The man was nowhere to be seen.

'You got to be kidding me,' Maple said, standing up and kicking the ground in frustration, angry that she'd missed her opportunity to get her bear back.

'Not so fast, Maple,' Mo said, pointing at a bulge protruding from underneath a pizza box on the ground near the bin. 'What's that?'

Maple walked towards the bin. She smiled when she removed the pizza box and saw what was on the ground. It was her bear.

'Yes!' she yelled, punching the air in delight. 'It must have fallen out of the man's backpack.'

She picked up the bear and brushed it off, before hugging it.

Its softness and smile made her happy and reminded her of better times.

'Mission accomplished,' Mo said, clapping his hands. 'That was simple. Now let's go back inside. It's getting cold out here.'

They turned around to go back inside the restaurant.

'Grrrrrrr!' a growling sound emerged from behind. They stood still.

'Grrrrrrrrrrrrrr!' the sound became louder, more aggressive.

They turned around, their legs shaking in fear, lips trembling.

A black Labrador emerged from a shadow. It was Sapper.

'Sapper,' Maple said. 'Is that you?'

The dog walked towards them with a stern look in its eyes.

Maple's heart raced as the dog walked within a few

feet of her. Sapper seemed to recognise the girl, with his tail now wagging and panting excitedly.

'Get back here, boy,' a deep voice called out from behind the shadow.

A large, tall and hairy looking man revealed himself. It was the same person they had seen trawling through the bin earlier.

Maple and Mo's faces turned white. They looked like they'd seen a ghost.

The man looked at Maple's hand and shook his head. His eyes filled with rage. 'What are you doing with my bear?' he yelled, pointing at it.

Maple's hands shook. 'It … it's my bear, actually,' she replied nervously.

The man walked slowly towards the pair. 'What are you talking about? It fell out of my backpack. It's mine.'

He was now one foot away from the pair, towering · over them.

'I … I … can explain,' she said, her body shaking, slowly taking a few steps back.

He was in no mood for talking. He reached out for the bear with his left hand and grabbed it from Maple.

Maple stood there in shock. It wasn't the action that scared her, it was something she saw on the man. He had a red poppy flower tattoo on his left hand.

She only knew one person in the whole world with that tattoo.

'What are you staring at, kid?'

'Dad. Is that you?'

He stood still, motionless.

He looked her in the eye. 'Maple,' he said, dropping the bear.

'No, it can't be,' he said, scratching his beard.

Mo looked on in astonishment.

He felt like he was sitting in the front row seat of a cinema, watching a thriller movie. The only thing missing was popcorn. He didn't dare say a word. His head moved from side to side like he was watching a tennis match as Maple and the man spoke to each other.

'It's me, Maple. That's my bear,' she said, pointing at the ground. 'I haven't seen you in ages. You look so different, like a wild animal with all that hair.'

The man felt uneasy. 'Yeah, I'm living a different life now. Not quite the same as before,' he said, taking a deep breath.

'I wish you didn't have to see me like this. I've changed a lot. I probably scare you.'

'Why don't you ever visit me and Mum? It's not like you've moved to a different state.'

The man felt anxious, his lips trembling. 'Look

Maple, it's not that simple. I'm not the same person I was. You and your mum are better off without me. I live on the streets now. You don't want to know me. It's a rough life.'

'Better off without us!' Maple exclaimed. 'Do you not realise how hard it has been since you've been gone? I'm one of the few kids at school without a dad. Do you have any idea how that makes me feel? What's wrong with you? What sort of dad abandons his family and doesn't even say goodbye? What changed you? What have you done to yourself?'

Maple began to cry. She couldn't understand why her dad didn't want to be in her life anymore. Why was he so different? What was wrong with him? It didn't seem fair.

'Look, take the bear. It's yours anyway,' the man said, handing her the toy. He was lost for words. He wanted to console his daughter, like he used to when she got upset.

'I wish I could explain, but you wouldn't understand. It's too complicated. You're too young.'

'Too complicated. Too young. What about Mum then? Is it too complicated for her as well? Is she too young?'

Tears flowed down her face.

'Don't go there, Maple. Now isn't the time to be

having this conversation.'

'Then when is a good time?'

The man stared at the darkening sky, wishing he was somewhere far away.

'Is everything alright out here?' a voice called out from the restaurant entrance.

Maple and Mo turned their heads. It was Mariam.

'Everything is fine, I was just on my way,' the man said. 'Come on, boy, let's go,' he said, grabbing Sapper by the collar.

The man and his dog took this distraction as an opportunity to run off down the alleyway and onto the beach boardwalk, out of sight.

Maple collapsed on the ground, holding her bear. She held it tightly.

Mariam and Mo rushed to her aid, kneeling beside her.

'What's wrong Maple? What happened? Did that man hurt you?' Mariam asked, placing her arm around Maple's shoulder.

Maple was too distraught to talk. She sat on the ground sobbing.

Mariam and Mo helped her up and brought her into the restaurant, sitting her down.

Maple and Mo sat beside each other, silently at the restaurant table. The silence was deafening.

Mo wanted to say something but didn't know what. He'd never been in a situation like this. He felt helpless. The girl he liked was in need of a friend and he could do nothing. It was as if their friendship had been fast forwarded a few years, with so much drama packed in a single day.

Mariam returned with two milkshakes.

'I'm not mopping this one up,' she said to Mo, who rolled his eyes.

'Now tell me what that was all about,' she said, looking at Maple. 'Why was that man talking to you?'

Maple paused. She stared at the milkshake. Her mind was filled with a mixture of emotions—anger and frustration, yet also relief and joy knowing that her dad was safe and okay.

'That was my dad,' she replied, her eyes red from crying.

'That man is your dad?' Mariam asked, looking confused.

'Yeah, you never said your dad wasn't living with you anymore,' Mo said, scratching his head. 'That hairy man is your dad? He looks homeless.'

'Don't be rude!' Mariam snapped. 'Never judge someone until you get to know them. You should know better.'

Maple took a slurp of the milkshake before

responding. It was the most difficult conversation she'd ever had to have.

'He lives on the streets now. He was in the army, but left when he came back from Afghanistan. Something changed him. He was a different person when he returned. He left Mum and me. We haven't seen him in a few years and now I find out he's homeless. I barely recognise him. I just don't get it.'

Mariam sat there in shock, feeling sorry for Maple.

'What did he do in the army and in Afghanistan?' she asked, hoping to learn more.

Maple rubbed her eyes. 'He was a combat engineer, helped clear explosives from the ground with the help of his dog.'

'His dog?' asked Mariam.

'The dog you just saw in the alleyway, the Labrador. His name is Sapper and he worked with my dad over there. Sapper would help sniff out the explosives and dad would remove them from the ground. Apparently he saved lots of lives.'

Mariam's mouth was wide open. Her heart raced.

'And you said your dad likes cricket?'

'That's right, and Sapper too,' replied Maple, unsure where the questioning was going.

'How do you know it's your dad given that man looks so different?' asked Mariam.

'He had my favourite teddy bear. I also recognised the poppy flower tattoo on his left hand.'

Mariam sat silent, her hands covering her mouth.

She couldn't believe what she was hearing. Her mind flooded with memories and emotions from her life back in Afghanistan.

The happiness that man brought to her and her family's life filled her with joy. That smile of his and kindness were forever ingrained in her mind.

He was one of the friendliest people she'd ever known.

Her last memory of him was the both of them enjoying their favourite sport – cricket.

Then the next day he was gone. Killed like so many other soldiers. A day that would forever change her family's life.

Hearing the news was one of the hardest days she'd ever experienced.

A friendship now just memories.

Or is he alive? she wondered.

'What is it, Mum?' Mo asked. His mother looked distressed, not her usual relaxed and composed self.

Mariam breathed heavily, unaware she was about to have one of the most difficult conversations of her life right there and then, with someone she only recently met.

'I know that man and that dog,' she replied, wiping

a tear from her eye. 'I knew them in Afghanistan.'

She placed her face in her hands and sobbed after saying those words. She never thought she would be talking about this man ever again. She thought he would only remain a memory.

Maple and Mo looked at each other, then at Mariam in disbelief. They couldn't believe what they were hearing.

CHAPTER 9

Mariam closed her eyes before speaking. She hadn't spoken of this moment in years. Especially not to any kids.

It was difficult to talk about. A day that would forever change her life.

She thought about Valour every day.

Her eyes opened. 'I know your dad,' she said, looking Maple in the eye. 'Mo's dad and I became close friends with him and his four-legged companion in Afghanistan. I thought he was dead.'

Maple's eyes locked with Mariam's. She barely blinked. Any surrounding sound from the restaurant was blocked out. Mariam had her undivided attention.

'What?' she asked. 'Dead!'

'Wait a minute, Mum,' Mo interrupted. 'You're telling us you know Maple's dad?'

Mariam nodded.

'That's right. I met him through Mo's dad, who was an interpreter attached to the Australian Army. He helped soldiers operate in villages through translation. We became close friends. Maple's dad taught me cricket as well. I used to only watch the game from the sidelines, but then got to play myself. He called me the princess of spin, as I was a good leg spin bowler. Despite all the challenges we went through over there, your dad was the ultimate optimist. Always had a smile on his face, always had a good attitude. He really inspired those around him.'

'You said you also know Sapper?' Maple asked.

Mariam smiled and giggled to herself. 'Oh yes, good old Sapper. Let's just say he's a multi-talented dog. He used to divide his time between sniffing out explosives and protecting us, and running away with cricket balls. He used to roll around a lot, begging for a belly scratch. Your dad used to say he spent most of his time dusting him off.'

Mo remained silent. He couldn't believe his classmate from school had a connection to his family. He also didn't realise how good his mum was at cricket. Princess of spin, he thought. Seriously? He thought the Warrior Beach Wombats were a social group for older ladies.

Mo hadn't heard his mum talk about his dad or Afghanistan for a long time.

'So what happened?' asked Maple. 'My dad seems the complete opposite now. Almost unrecognisable. He looks scary.'

Mariam took a deep breath. This was a difficult

conversation. She paused before speaking. 'There was an accident,' she said. Her lips trembled as she said those four words. A part of her felt like she was doing the children a disservice. As a mother, she saw herself as a protector and guardian.

This conversation would be brutal.

Maple and Mo looked at her attentively, their eyes fixed on Mariam's. Nothing else in the world mattered to them at that moment. It was as if they were learning more about their soul each time her lips moved.

'What sort of accident?' Maple asked.

Tears filled Mariam's eyes. She looked around the restaurant. A few metres away, a father sat opposite his young son and daughter, enjoying a meal together. They were laughing about something. The father was reading a card his kids had given him.

She didn't know what they were laughing about, but she was almost certain they weren't talking about something as life changing as this.

She loved her homeland but sometimes she wished she was born here instead. How many struggles and problems could have been avoided by growing up in Australia?

She turned to face Maple and Mo. 'Mo's dad and soldiers from your dad's army unit were tasked with searching a nearby village for explosives in the ground one day. It was a stinking hot day, over forty degrees. It felt like an oven. I was there dropping food off to some friends. It all changed in a few seconds.'

Mariam paused and stopped talking. Her mind was overcome with thoughts and emotions.

'Please keep going,' Maple begged.

'Yeah, Mum, this is important,' pleaded Mo.

Mariam collected her thoughts and continued speaking. 'One moment the soldiers were searching the ground and the next we heard a loud bang. There was a lot of commotion in the village. No one knew what was going on. People were running around frantically, trying to find out more. It was chaos. Adults and children were crying and shaking. Some people were hurt. I had Mo with me and tried to remain calm. Then a military helicopter arrived and disappeared shortly after. It was all over so quickly. I was told later that day that Mo's dad had died in the explosion, along with three others in the village and an Australian soldier. I always assumed it was Maple's dad as they said he was the dog handler. I never heard from him again. It was the worst day of my life. I remember collapsing on the ground and sobbing all night. My life was shattered. I never saw my husband or your dad again, Maple. Just like that I was a single mum with an uncertain future. Few prospects. I think about them both every day. They were my heroes, my inspiration. Nothing can prepare you for a moment like that. It feels like someone has kicked you in the guts.'

'What happened after that?' asked Mo.

'You don't have to answer that,' Maple interjected. 'This isn't an easy conversation. We can always continue it another time if you prefer.'

'No, no it's okay,' Mariam said.

'It's an important part of our journey. I didn't expect to survive very long. I was sure the Taliban would come back and finish us off. I stayed in the village another day and then packed up and set off with Mo and a few other families. Each day was filled with uncertainty. Some days we were able to stay with relatives, while other days we were forced to sleep rough on the street. I feel ashamed that I had to put my son through that.'

Mo's eyes filled with tears.

'You're the bravest woman I've ever met,' Maple said, putting an arm around her. 'I'm not as brave as you. My heroes have always been athletes and musicians. I'm sitting right next to a real hero.'

Mariam stroked Maple's hand. 'That's very kind of you dear. But how am I a hero? I didn't save any lives.'

Mariam choked up and began crying, her head facing the table. Maple and Mo each placed an arm on her shoulder, trying to console her.

'You saved his,' Maple said, pointing at Mo.

'If it weren't for your strength of character and love, who knows what could have happened to you. How did you end up in Australia?'

'We moved around for a few years after the accident. I never felt safe. I was always looking over my shoulder. Then one day we met an Australian aid worker who told us about the humanitarian visa program. Thankfully we qualified and a few months later we boarded a plane and arrived in Warrior Beach. We've been here ever since.'

'What was it like moving here?' asked Maple.

'It was harder than it sounds. People think because Australia is such a rich, prosperous country, then it must be simple. It wasn't. We were faced with a whole new culture, new systems and everything. It was like starting all over again. But getting on that plane was the best decision I ever made.'

'Why is that?' asked Maple.

'Australia is filled with opportunity. I can work and support my family. Mo can go to school, dream big and achieve his goals through hard work. None of that could be guaranteed back in Afghanistan. We are also safe here. We don't have to look over our shoulders anymore.'

'How is it you risk everything to save your family

and yet my dad who lives in this land of opportunity wants nothing to do with me and my mum?' Maple asked, shaking her head in anger. 'It doesn't make sense.'

Although Mariam's story inspired her, it also reminded her of what she was missing – her dad. Why was he able to risk his life saving people in Afghanistan, but couldn't even save his own family back home? Why does putting on a camouflage uniform make a difference?

Mariam held Maple's hands.

'It's not that simple, my dear,' she said. 'He loves you, trust me. Being a soldier is a tough business. They suffer too. Not just over there. When they return home as well. Although your dad did amazing things, he had friends die over there and others got injured. That stuff can haunt you. They're called invisible wounds. Wounds you can't see. I wish I could see your dad again, Maple. It would mean everything.'

'That could be hard,' Maple said. 'He's homeless and constantly moving. Plus, I don't think he wants to see me again. He made it pretty clear earlier that he wants to be left alone. He is probably heading as far away from here as he can to avoid another confrontation.'

All three sat silent and still for what felt like an

eternity. The world as they knew it had been flipped upside down.

Maple missed her dad. It was all starting to make sense. This explained a lot. Going through a trauma like that and carrying those memories with you every day must be hard. She wondered if she would ever see him again.

She felt bad for harbouring resentment towards him.

Mo was also overcome with thoughts. He'd just learnt more about his dad in a few minutes than at any time during his life. It was hard for him to digest all the information.

Their thoughts were interrupted by a growling sound outside the restaurant.

'Woooooofffff!' barked a dog near the entrance.

Maple turned around and saw a familiar sight sitting just outside – it was Sapper.

'Shhhhhh,' Maple hissed, feeling a bit embarrassed.

'Grrrrrrrr!' Sapper's growl became louder like a jack hammer.

'What are you doing here Sapper?' asked Maple.

'I think he's trying to tell us something,' Mo said.

'Let's go find out,' Mariam insisted.

All three walked outside to see what all the fuss was about.

Sapper walked a few metres towards the boardwalk, as if he was trying to lead them somewhere.

'I think he wants to take us somewhere,' Mariam said.

'Maybe he knows where your dad is, Maple,' Mo said.

'Only one way to find out. Let's follow him,' said Maple, determined to find her dad and reunite Mariam with him.

CHAPTER 10

The trio followed Sapper along the beach boardwalk. The sight of them following the dog resembled that of a shepherd leading his flock through a paddock.

Sapper walked with his tongue hanging out of his mouth, tail wagging. Unlike the others who appeared frantic and stressed, he was relaxed, cool as a cucumber.

The boardwalk was still buzzing with life that evening.

Mariam looked at the time on her mobile phone – it was 5.50pm.

Sapper kept his distance from them.

'You do realise we're following a dog?' asked Mo, wondering where they were being led, as they dodged in-between people. The fast-paced walking caused his upper body to break out in a sweat. He knew he should have applied deodorant after going to the beach. Now he risked overwhelming his new friend with unpleasant body odour.

'Shhhh!' Mariam snapped. 'You don't know Sapper like I do. This is no ordinary dog. He's a warrior. It's like he has a built-in compass in his head. Not to mention his sense of smell. He can sniff out a target from afar. We may not even be alive today or living in Australia if it weren't for this courageous dog.'

Maple and Mo looked at each other in amazement.

Sapper led them down a set of stairs leading to the beach.

They removed their shoes and walked on the warm sand, against the sound of waves crashing on the shoreline.

The air was warm and smelt of sea salt. Seagulls congregated in packs, on the lookout for leftover food.

Sapper barked at a solitary figure he spotted in the distance, sitting alone on the sand.

He sprinted towards the figure, his short legs kicking up sand with every stride.

'It must be him!' yelled Maple.

They chased after Sapper.

They caught up to Sapper about a minute later, who was sitting down next to the lone figure. They stood still, arms on their waists, huffing and puffing, their faces covered in sweat.

Maple walked in front of the man and looked in his face. The man looked back at her.

It was her dad.

He didn't speak, just continued to look out at the ocean, distracted by the waves and seagulls.

'Dad, it's me, Maple,' she said, puffing and kneeling

down beside him, waving her arms in his face.

Valour's face remained expressionless. He grabbed a handful of sand in his right hand, slowly releasing it.

'Come on guys, let's sit down for a bit,' Mariam said. She was filled with adrenalin. Years of heartache and agony had been lifted from her shoulders.

All three sat down on the sand, with Mariam and Mo sitting a few metres behind Valour.

No one dared speak. They sat still, taking in the ocean's sounds – the thunderous roar of the swell, and the milk-like whitewash, made it look like one of the most exhilarating and scary places to be at the same time. A place where you could be free from life's dramas, and at peace with yourself.

Valour looked at Maple. 'I take it Sapper led you to me,' he said, giving his furry friend a pat on the head and a look of disapproval.

'Some people just want to be left alone, don't want to be found. Why don't you go home to Mum and leave me here? It's getting late. She's probably worried about you.'

'We wanted to see you again,' Maple said, wiping sweat from her forehead. 'This is my friend Mo and his mum. Mo's mum told me a lot about you. I get it. I understand a bit more about what you're going through.'

'Get what?' Valour asked, surprised, turning around to look at Mo and Mariam. The boy looked unfamiliar, while his mother resembled that of an old friend.

'Why you're upset. I heard the story about what happened that day in Afghanistan.'

Valour ground his teeth and clenched the sand with his fists in anger.

'What would you know? You're just a kid,' he said, raising his voice. 'What do you mean, this woman told you things about me? What would she know? Who is she anyway?'

Maple felt a shiver go down her spine. She felt uneasy, unsure of what to do. She looked down at the sand for answers.

Mariam sensed Maple's uneasiness and intervened.

'It's me, Mariam,' she said, smiling at Valour.

Valour looked at her. 'Who?' he asked.

'Mariam from Afghanistan. You remember the princess of spin? You taught me cricket. You worked with my husband, who was an interpreter attached to your army unit.'

Valour's eyes widened. What was happening? he wondered. He thought he must be imagining things.

'Don't be ridiculous,' he said. 'I don't know what game you're playing, but that man and his family passed away a long time ago.'

'I'm not kidding,' Mariam said. 'Look me in the eye.' Mariam crawled closer to Valour, their faces only inches apart.

Valour stared into her eyes. His jaw dropped and heart sank as he saw the one green, one brown eye. It was really her.

He began to breathe heavily.

'How is this possible, how can you be here right now? I thought you and your son passed away in the explosion that day like your husband,' he said, his arms tucked around his head, biting his bottom lip.

Mariam grabbed his left hand, recognising the poppy flower tattoo. 'I survived,' she replied, a tear running down her cheek.

'So did my son, Mohammed.'

'What?' exclaimed Valour.

Mariam pointed towards Mo, who looked back at Valour, smiling.

'This is Mo. He's now sixteen, like Maple. We live here now. We moved over a number of years ago. He goes to school with your daughter. It's so good to see you. All this time I thought you had died that day.'

Valour was speechless and fell on his back, staring at the evening sky. The pain and suffering he endured over the past many years were now being combined with a sense of confusion, happiness and joy.

Memories from his time in Afghanistan flooded his mind.

He felt like a heavy load had been lifted from his shoulders. Anger was replaced by a sense of relief and happiness.

'So what happened to you then?' he asked. 'The army told me you died in the explosion.'

Mariam wiped away her tears before speaking. 'The explosion didn't hurt me. I was out delivering food to a friend, but I left the village shortly after and never returned, which is probably why we never saw each other again. A few years later we were offered the chance to move to Australia and start a new life. It was a dream come true.'

'What happened to you, my friend?' quizzed Mariam. 'I thought you were the soldier who died that day while on patrol.'

'No, it was Jimmy,' Valour said, looking down at the sand.

'How is that possible? You told me the day before the accident when we were playing cricket that you would be the one who would be out on patrol.'

Valour looked back up at the sky for answers, before looking Mariam in the eyes.

'He took my place that day. I was unwell and

couldn't go out. It was supposed to be a simple patrol. It turned into a disaster.'

Valour's face wore a sombre look. 'I still feel guilty. I should have been there that day, helping the other soldiers. Sapper was the best explosive detection dog and would have detected the explosives before it was too late. He couldn't join them because I'm his handler and trained to be with him. It's my fault what happened and it's definitely my fault Jimmy died.'

Mariam leaned forward and put her arm around his shoulder. 'It's not your fault Valour. Think of all the other lives you saved when you were over there. All the other bombs you and Sapper found. Because of your courage and actions, countless people in Afghanistan can live safer, better lives. You're a hero.'

Valour rested his head against Mariam's shoulder, his eyes filled with tears. 'I don't feel like a hero. If I'm a hero, then why does it hurt so much? Why am I such a terrible husband and father?'

Mariam stroked his hair. 'Wars and violence can torture people's minds. It's not fair. I have tough moments too. Just take it day by day.'

'I think you're a hero,' Mo said.

'Me too,' agreed Maple.

Valour wiped his eyes, stood up and brushed the sand off. He walked up to Mo. 'It's so good to meet you,' Valour said, holding out his hand. The two shook hands, followed by Valour giving him a hug.

'Your dad was a great man,' he whispered in his ear. 'He died protecting you, your mum and his village. There's so much about him I want to share with you.'

Tears filled Mo's eyes. It was the happiest he'd been in a long time.

'We considered your dad one of us. He possessed all the values of an Australian soldier – courage, strength and mateship. He was one of the best people I ever served with. You should be proud of him and learn about his legacy.'

Maple and Mariam stood up and walked towards them.

'I know you've been struggling,' Mariam said to Valour. 'I want to help. It's the least I can do given everything you've done for my family.'

'I'm a different person now, Mariam. A lot has changed since the war. Just look at me. I look like a wild animal, living on the streets. You don't want to know me.'

'It's what's in here that counts,' Mariam said, pointing to her heart. 'You have a family that love you and miss you. You just need to take it one step at a time.'

Valour looked at Maple. Milestones he'd shared

with her in the past filled his mind – from the first time he held her after she was born, her first birthday and teaching her how to body board. He regretted the milestones he'd missed since leaving.

'I don't know, Mariam. I'm damaged goods now. I'm broken and I don't think I can be put back together that easily.'

'That's not the Valour I know,' Mariam said. 'The Valour I know wouldn't back down from a challenge. He would find a way through. The Valour I know wouldn't leave a mission incomplete. The Valour I know …'

'The mission is over,' Valour interrupted. 'It's over and I lost. I lost my friends, your husband.'

'Soldiers shouldn't just worry about the battlefront,' Mariam said. 'They should also worry about the home front. That's your mission now. Your family. Am I right?'

He nodded.

'One day at a time,' Mariam said.

'You're right as always,' he replied. 'Seeing you again and meeting Mo has given me so much hope. I don't know how I'll do it but I owe it to Abdul, Jimmy and you guys to try at least.'

'Talking about the home front' said Mo, 'I met a young girl today whose dad also served in the

Afghanistan War with the Australian Army. But he was unfortunately killed over there. She's quite inspiring–helps out a lot at home with chores and looks after her brother a lot.'

Valour looked at him inquisitively. 'We lost a lot of great soldiers over there. You don't happen to know his name, do you? I might know someone who served with him.'

'I didn't get his name, but her name is Vicky Jacobs.'

Valour froze, his face expressionless.

'What's wrong?' Mo asked.

'I can't believe what's happening. I'll explain it later.'

He looked down at Maple, placing his arms on her shoulders. 'I'm sorry, Maple. I wish I could have been there for you these last few years. I promise I will try to be a better dad and make it up to you and your mum. It won't be easy, but I'll try my hardest.'

'It's okay, Dad,' Maple said, tears flowing down her cheeks. 'You don't have to apologise.'

All four embraced each other, hugging in a circle. Sapper snuck his way into the middle, barking furiously in delight.

'Are you still playing cricket, Mariam?' asked Valour.

Mariam laughed. 'Sure am, you should come and

watch me play. I'm still the princess of spin. I even passed on those tricks you taught me to Mo.'

'I'd like that,' replied Valour, who now wore a broad smile across his face.

A humming sound approached from above. They looked up at the sky. It was the same military helicopter as before. Its camouflage colours reminded them all of the sacrifices made by our servicemen and women, and their families.

Despite their different backgrounds, the four of them shared an unbreakable bond and connection, forged through courage and overcoming adversity.

'Unconquered,' Mariam said to Valour. 'That was the last thing Abdul said about you before he left home that day for the last time. You're unconquered.'

'We all are,' replied Valour. 'We're the captains of our souls.'

EPILOGUE

Valour splashed his face with water. His eyes remained shut as the water dripped down his nose and cheeks and into the sink.

He opened one eye and watched as the water ran down the drain. A part of him wanted to disappear down the drain. Be somewhere else.

Sapper wasn't there. Stevie agreed to look after him that afternoon.

He was alone inside the men's bathroom. A light bulb above flickered.

The bathroom stalls were peppered with graffiti.

'Warrior Beach High School. Hasn't changed bit,' he said, shaking his head.

He breathed slowly. Today was a test. He felt numb. He still wasn't used to big crowds. They made him anxious and nervous.

His thoughts were interrupted by the buzzing sound of his mobile phone. He'd received a text message. It read:

Hi Dad, so glad you could make it today. I'll look out for you in the crowd. It means a lot having you here. Hope you enjoy it. We'll catch up afterwards.

Love Maple xox

He didn't respond. Valour stared at himself in the mirror, reflecting on the last two years.

He grabbed the side of the sink with both hands.

His face was clean-shaven. He ran his hands through his short hair.

His shirt was neatly tucked into his trousers, with the sleeves rolled up. His brown leather shoes were polished.

He looked like the old Valour, but still didn't feel like the old Valour inside.

'You can do this. Do it for Maple,' he whispered to himself.

His life had been a rollercoaster since that unofficial reunion on the beach that December evening.

One step at a time, he promised them. That's exactly what he delivered.

Some days it was two steps forward and one step back, while other days it was the opposite. He liked to think he'd taken more steps forward than backwards.

At least he was spending more time with his family and less time on the streets.

Over the past month he'd slept under the same roof as Veronica and Maple five days.

Although he was always drawn back to the stars. It provided him with peace.

Reuniting with Veronica and Maple after so long

was the hardest thing he'd ever done. It took him months to summon the courage to walk through the front door of their home again. It was overwhelming.

They initially met at a local park and just sat and talked, sometimes for hours.

Sometimes they looked each other in the eyes when they spoke, while other times they looked straight ahead.

Over time, the smiles increased and the arguing decreased.

It wasn't perfect. They knew that. Maybe it never would be again. Time can't heal all wounds, but it can help repair them.

He'd started speaking to a psychologist.

Mariam had also been a huge help. Catching up with her regularly helped with his invisible wounds.

He encouraged Maple to take up soccer again, which she did. He even attended some of her games.

Valour retrieved an envelope from his right pocket and pulled out a letter. It was the letter Mariam's husband, Abdul, had written to him the day before the accident.

He'd never read it. Now seemed like an appropriate time, given the anguish he was going through.

He unfolded the letter slowly. His heart raced as words appeared.

My dear friend, Valour,

Writing this letter has provided me with so much gratitude and appreciation.
The kindness and sincerity you have shown my family and our village cannot be understated. You are the kindest person I have ever met.
You and your team have made our community safer, which has allowed all of us to enjoy greater freedoms.
The way you have accepted me into your team is something I don't take for granted.
I hope we can remain friends beyond this war and stay in touch.
If there's ever a time in your life when you feel alone or are struggling, my family is there with you.
We won't forget you.

Yours sincerely,
Abdul

Valour folded the letter and put it back in his pocket. He grabbed the sides of the sink firmly, as the tears flowed down his cheeks.

Memories of his time with Abdul and his family ran through his mind.

He missed his friend. There was only one Abdul.

Valour looked at the time on his phone. It was 2.30pm. He needed to take his seat.

He wiped his face and left the bathroom, where he was met by Veronica and Mariam.

'You ready for this?' Veronica asked, as she adjusted his shirt collar.

'I guess so,' he replied, taking a deep breath.

'We're here for you, every step of the way,' Mariam said, smiling.

The three of them walked into the school assembly hall. It was packed like a crowd before a sports game. Hundreds of parents and kids everywhere, chatting away. The students' uniforms looked unusually well ironed and neat.

Lions, zebras, gazelles and giraffes together under the same roof.

Veronica grabbed Valour's left hand and guided him to their seat, about ten rows back from the stage.

They sat silently waiting for the ceremony to begin.

The roar of the audience subsided as soon as the principal appeared, walking down the aisle.

He was followed by a conga line of senior staff and some students.

Valour glanced at the delegation as they walked onto the stage. He turned his head away, then immediately back at the stage.

Maple and Mo were on stage. He closed his eyes, wondering what on earth was happening.

Maple and Mo took their seats on either side of the principal, looking out towards the crowd. The crowd cast their eyes on them like crows sussing out food.

They were both nervous. Maple's knees shook slightly in anticipation.

The next half hour was spent listening to a speech from the principal and watching selected students from Year 12 receive awards, including Mo who was unsurprisingly awarded Dux.

Following the awards ceremony, the principal approached the lectern.

Maple clenched her fists.

'I now have the pleasure of calling to the lectern a remarkable student to say a few words. She is the recipient of this year's Resilience Award. Please give a warm welcome to our school vice-captain, Maple,' he said, clapping his hands.

The crowd clapped even louder. It was thunderous.

Maple walked slowly to the lectern and unwrapped a prepared speech.

All eyes were on her.

She cleared her throat before speaking.

'My fellow classmates,

I know you're itching to race out of those gates for

the last time, so I'll keep this short.

These last few years have been a bit up and down for me. Okay, I'll be honest, they've been an absolute rollercoaster.

Two years ago, I was down and out. I didn't even know if I'd finish school, let alone speak in front of my entire class.

Nothing was working for me. I was unhappy at home, unhappy at school and I disengaged from anyone wanting to support me.

I wanted to escape but didn't know how. I was screaming inside.

I'd gone from being such a driven, confident young woman to being insular and down and out. I was counting down until my last day at school, when I could finally be free. This place felt like a prison, rather than a school, with inmates rather than students.

Then on one December evening after school my life changed.

I learnt more about my family and my community in those few hours than ever before.

It was a transformative moment in my life.

It taught me a lot about the power of humanity, resilience and sacrifice. These aren't just words, they are actions and ideals that enable people to overcome all kinds of challenges and struggles.

It also taught me about loss. You don't need someone in your life to die to think you've lost them. Sometimes it feels like their soul has disappeared.

My message to all of you is: don't judge someone until you understand their soul. Some of the greatest people in our community are the ones struggling the most. They need our understanding and respect.

Too often I think we judge a book by its cover, when we should look deeper than that. We need to look at their character, their values, because that it what truly defines all of us – not what we wear or the music we listen to.

I made a promise to myself after that evening to change my life and try to be a better person. It started at home, helping Mum more around the house, but also reconnecting with my dad, who I grew up worshipping.

Change doesn't happen overnight. You need to take it step by step, day by day.

That's what I did. I slowly began to reconnect with the things that make me happy and bring a smile to my face.

I encourage you all to do the same. Work out what makes you happy and what makes you smile. Once you've done that, life will take care of the rest.

We all have a purpose, we all have a gift. We just need to nurture it.

I will conclude by reading a poem which changed my life. It's called Invictus by William Ernest Henley.

Out of the night that covers me,
Black as the pit from pole to pole,
I thank whatever gods may be
For my unconquerable soul.

In the fell clutch of circumstance
I have not winced nor cried aloud.
Under the bludgeonings of chance
My head is bloody, but unbowed.

Beyond this place of wrath and tears
Looms but the Horror of the shade,
And yet the menace of the years
Finds and shall find me unafraid.

It matters not how strait the gate,
How charged with punishments the scroll,
I am the master of my fate,
I am the captain of my soul.

Let us remember, we are the captains of our souls. No matter how tough life can be, how cruel the circumstances, we are unconquerable.

Thank you.'

Maple turned around and walked back to her seat. The crowd stood in ovation, cheering. A rare moment in which all students were united. Her story resonated with them.

Her face turned pink from the attention.

Maple gazed across the hall like a bird looking for its prey. She desperately wanted to see him.

She was about to give up, then she saw her dad. He was standing, wiping away tears with his right hand, while his left arm was around Veronica's shoulders.

He looked proud.

Maple felt a buzz in her skirt pocket. She'd received a text message on her mobile phone.

It read:

That was amazing, sweetie, so proud of you. You inspire me. Love Mo xox

Maple leaned forward and turned to the right towards her boyfriend, blowing him a kiss.

A couple of minutes later the principal returned to the lectern.

'Thank you, Maple, that was beautiful,' he said.

'Before we conclude today's graduation, I'd like to invite our school captain, Mo, to the stage to provide closing remarks.'

The crowd clapped as he approached the lectern.

He walked in a more sophisticated manner now, less Olympian, more statesman like.

His face was clean-shaven.

He looked out at the crowd. He didn't have a prepared speech. He spoke off the cuff.

'Friends, classmates, staff,

I take this opportunity not to talk about myself, but to focus on those in my life who have made me the man I am today.

You know who you are – teachers, coaches, even my mum.

My journey to this country wasn't easy. Many years ago, when I was little, my mum risked everything so I could enjoy a better life. And because of all those who believed in me, I've been able to achieve my dreams.

I owe this place a debt of gratitude. It's changed my life.

I want to say thank you.

Thank you for always looking out for me.

Thank you for believing in me when I didn't even believe in myself. Thank you for the sacrifices you've made for me.

I would like to give a special shout out to one particular staff member–the school counsellor, Mr Fredericks.

A couple of years ago, Mr Fredericks invited me to

be part of a mentoring program, where I was paired up with a Year 7 student.

I thought it was going to be boring and a complete waste of time.

Little did I know the impact it would have on my life.

That day I was paired with then Year 7 student, Vicky. She's now a pimple-faced, much taller Year 9 student.

Vicky is one of the most enthusiastic, empathetic people I've ever met. I'm proud to call her my friend.

She broadened my perspective on life.

Vicky – I know you're in the crowd today, probably wondering why Mr Fredericks insisted you attend today's graduation.

This is why. Thank you for being you. You've got three more years left at this school, and the school will be better for it.

I conclude my speech with this message for all Year 12 students – be grateful for what you have and make a difference whatever you choose to do.

Life isn't about money and power. It's bigger than that. It's about community and family. At the end of the day, without those two things, we don't exist.

And have a bit of fun in between. You can't take life too seriously. You need to laugh as well.

On that note, I say farewell to this special place. It's

been fun.

Thank you.'

Most of the crowd roared in delight like the roar of soccer fans after a player scores the winning goal in extra time. Some students waved their arms in delight, with others whistling.

The words inspired them.

Other students gazed at the time on their phones, desperate to leave.

Each student there had their own story. Some stories contained more laughter than others, while others had too many tears and heartache.

Some would go on to university and realise their family's ambitions for them. Some would struggle, unable to cope with life's growing demands.

It took a few minutes for the cheers to end, before the principal could say one final farewell.

The crowd dispersed in all directions. The sight was akin to herds of cattle roaming a paddock.

Maple and Mo jumped off the stage and ran to their families, who remained seated.

They exchanged hugs with each other.

'I'm so proud of you,' Valour said, while embracing his daughter.

'Thank you, Dad, I love you.'

Maple and Mo looked at each other. They were both excited and scared about what lay ahead in the future.

Mo hoped to study mechanical engineering at university, while Maple dreamed of studying psychology. Their final marks would arrive in a couple of weeks.

The five of them left the school and walked back to their cars. The sky was bright blue.

Valour left holding his wife's hand, feeling good and happy that he'd attended.

Although he didn't know whether he would be sleeping in a bed or under the stars tonight, he could at least go to sleep knowing he was bringing smiles to his wife and daughter's faces.

The group never took moments like this with Valour for granted. This was a good day.

Valour looked up at the sky, hoping his mates were looking down on him.

His soul was healing. One day at a time.